She Could Climb Trees, Play Football, Talk Cars And Quote Sports Statistics With The Best Of Them. And If The Need Arose, She Knew How To Fell A Man With One Quick Move.

What she hadn't quite mastered, though, was how a woman could resist when the man she'd wanted for years was so close she could lift her lips and touch her mouth to his.

With every fiber of her being, she yearned to move against him, rest her head on his shoulder and feel his big masculine arms enfold her. But that was exactly why she couldn't.

Any notion she'd ever had of snagging Sam had disappeared when she'd embarrassed herself with a youthful, impassioned declaration that was ill-timed to say the least. Sam might pretend he'd only been letting her down easy, but she had a hunch that in their charged encounter way back then, he had been speaking the truth.

Sam's perfect woman was not Annalise. Not by a long shot.

Dear Reader,

When I set out to write Annalise's story, I knew she would be someone special. I also realized that her hero needed to be a man who could see past her outer shell of wealth and beauty to the sometimes emotionally fragile woman within.

Annalise fascinated me as she came to life on the page. She and I have very little in common. So I had to stretch my limits to understand this complex sister/daughter/cousin.

After growing up on Wolff Mountain amid an incredible sea of testosterone, Annalise had to learn (as an adult) what it meant to be a woman. Not a carbon copy of anyone else…but simply herself. A still-sore memory from her past puts the lone female Wolff's unexpected chance to find a mate in jeopardy.

Sam and Annalise strike sparks off one another. Come along and see what happens when two strong-willed people go head-to-head and happen to fall in love when they least expect it.

Happy reading,

Janice Maynard

www.JaniceMaynard.com
www.WolffMountain.com

JANICE MAYNARD

ALL GROWN UP

HARLEQUIN®
entertain, enrich, inspire™

Recycling programs
for this product may
not exist in your area.

ISBN-13: 978-0-373-73219-7

ALL GROWN UP

Books by Janice Maynard

Harlequin Desire

The Billionaire's Borrowed Baby #2109
*Into His Private Domain #2135
*A Touch of Persuasion #2146
*Impossible to Resist #2164
*The Maid's Daughter #2182
*All Grown Up #2206

Silhouette Desire

The Secret Child & the Cowboy CEO #2040

*The Men of Wolff Mountain

Other titles by this author available in ebook format.

JANICE MAYNARD

came to writing early in life. When her short story *The Princess and the Robbers* won a red ribbon in her third-grade school arts fair, Janice was hooked. She holds a B.A. from Emory and Henry College and an M.A. from East Tennessee State University. In 2002 Janice left a fifteen-year career as an elementary teacher to pursue writing full-time. Her first love is creating sexy, character-driven, contemporary romance. She has written for Kensington and NAL, and now is so very happy to also be part of the Harlequin Books family—a lifelong dream, by the way!

Janice and her husband live in beautiful east Tennessee in the shadow of the Great Smoky Mountains. She loves to travel and enjoys using those experiences as settings for books.

Hearing from readers is one of the best perks of the job! Visit her website, www.janicemaynard.com, or email her at JESM13@aol.com. And of course, don't forget Facebook and don't forget Facebook and Twitter. Visit all the men of Wolff Mountain at www.wolffmountain.com.

This book is dedicated to women everywhere
who pave their own way with grace and beauty
and originality. Never apologize for being who you are.
Life has shaped you with experiences both good and bad.
Embrace your unique self and let the world
know what you have to offer. Shine!

One

Annalise Wolff regarded Sam Ely much like she did the IRS. She was forced to deal with him occasionally, but the experience inevitably gave her a bad feeling in the pit of her stomach…thus making her voluntary presence in his office today all the more incomprehensible. She leaned back in her chair, crossed one slim leg over the other and admired the sheen on her soft ebony leather boots. They were Prada, as was her voluminous purse.

Suffering the indignity of face-to-face contact with the ridiculously handsome architect required full body armor. Her crimson cashmere sweater and narrow black wool skirt were designed to show him she was all grown up.

Unfortunately, Sam didn't seem all that impressed.

He lounged against the window frame, his gaze absently focused on the wintry day outside. "Yes or no, Annalise," he said, a faint but unmistakable bite in his voice despite his honeyed drawl. "I'm giving you the courtesy of first refusal, but there are dozens of interior designers who would jump at this opportunity."

He was right, damn his scurvy, sexy, Southern hide. The Shenandoah Valley home and dairy farm that belonged to his grandparents dated back to the time of Thomas Jefferson. The house was listed on the national register. Experts in historic renovation were handling the extensive changes Sam had drawn in detail via the plans rolled out on a nearby table. The project was an interior designer's dream. She stalled, telling herself she could walk away. "And the magazine spread afterward is a done deal?"

"My college roommate's mom is the managing editor of *Architectural Design*. She's salivating at the opportunity to put Sycamore Farm in the earliest possible issue. The only holdup at the moment is you."

He returned to his desk and sat down on the edge of it, his long, muscular legs dangerously close to hers. The position put him above her, and she knew he did it deliberately. She'd known this man for most of her life. His father had done the architectural design for much of Wolff Castle, and Sam and his dad had been frequent visitors to the Wolff home over the years. For an adolescent girl locked away like Rapunzel in her tower, Annalise's interactions with the much older Sam had been her first and only exposure to hormonal-driven, adolescent passion.

"When would I start?" she hedged. "If I agree."

He glanced down at the calendar beside him. "I'm sure you have a few things to wrap up. How about a week from Friday? Gram and Pops want you to live onsite, given the remoteness of the farm. Too much time commuting would eat into the schedule."

She felt her face heat. "Where will you be?"

He put his hands on his thighs, drawing her attention to their size and firmness and the shape of his masculinity nestled where they met. "Don't worry," he muttered, irritation etching a scowl between his eyebrows as he glared at her. "Gram wants me to spend a couple of days at the beginning to orient you to the project, but afterward, I'll return here to my office, far, far, away. That should put your mind at rest." He ran a hand through his hair. "For God's sake, I'm not making you a prisoner. Go home whenever you need to, but I want you to give this job a hundred and ten percent. Or nothing."

He sat up, back straight, arms folded, eyes glittering with challenge. "Do I make you nervous, Annalise?"

"Of course not." Her reply was commendably quick, but lamentably false. "I'm just not sure if I have the time to fit you into my schedule." Annalise didn't need the money. But the cachet of having her name on this massive undertaking would take her business and reputation to a whole new level. She was ambitious, damn it. Sam might not think of her as anything more than a family friend, but professionally he had her pegged.

He took her hand and drew her to her feet, cradling her loosely in the vee of his legs. "Make time, Annalise," he said, his gaze locking onto hers like a charlatan preparing to hypnotize an unwary victim. "You know you want to."

Sam was overplaying his hand. Sexual nuance was not his normal mode of doing business. But the God's honest truth was, Annalise made *him* nervous. He'd hurt her badly seven years ago when she'd had a big crush on him, and though he'd like to believe that was water under the bridge, the wariness in her sooty-lashed, pale blue eyes was unmistakable. The adoration she'd showered him with so long ago had changed into fury the instant he'd rejected her, and she had never forgiven him.

The reluctant attraction he battled even now had sim-

mered back then. He'd never been able to forget what
happened, and though he'd tried on several occasions to
apologize over the years, Annalise shut him down time and
again until he finally gave up and avoided her as much as
possible. She did likewise.

But like a stubborn splinter beneath the skin, he couldn't
seem to extract her from his life and his thoughts. So when
his grandparents insisted he offer the job to Annalise, he'd
relished the opportunity to get her alone, to invite her to
his office, to see her face-to-face.

The color of her irises was unusual for a woman with
hair so dark and glossy. But then again, most everything
about Annalise Wolff was extraordinary. Tall and slim and
infinitely confident, her striking looks could have made
her a runway model or a film star. She carried herself
with a boldness that did nothing to minimize her intense
femininity.

For a split second, Sam allowed himself to imagine
all that boundless energy and subtle sexual aggression in
his bed. His sex hardened to the point of pain. This was
why he normally kept a healthy distance. He didn't want
to think of her that way. Cursing his own stupidity, he set
her aside and put the desk between them. "I can't give you
long to make up your mind. Gram wanted you because of
the work you did on the president's home at UVA. She and
my grandfather attended the reception that showcased the
renovations there and they were both very impressed with
your work. But if you don't have the time, just say so."

Annalise folded her arms beneath her breasts. The soft
red sweater she wore delineated her modest curves and
her narrow waist. Sam had big hands, and it was not a far
stretch to imagine himself lifting her and spreading her
legs and—

Oh, hell.

She tilted her chin upward, nose in the air. "You'd like that, wouldn't you? But sorry, Sam Ely, I guess you're stuck with me. If your grandmother wants me to do this project, I'm in."

The jolt of joy that stabbed through his chest was a surprise. Did he really want an excuse to spend time with the prickly, stubborn Annalise Wolff? Apparently, according to his unreasonable but insistent erection, he did.

Sam cleared his throat, making a show of turning the calendar around and jotting a note. "I'll get my attorney to draw up a contract. Do you have any questions?"

Ten days later, Annalise steered her Miata along a narrow paved road that led up to the entrance of Sycamore Farm. In the dead of winter, the property was not all that impressive. Fallow fields crusted with frost flanked both sides of the road. Excessive freezing and thawing had played havoc with the asphalt, leaving the occasional pothole.

Sam's grandparents had been gone for several weeks, searching out warmer climes. But Annalise had been assured that the fridge and pantry were stocked and at least one bedroom outfitted for a long-term guest.

Remembering her last encounter with Sam, she muttered an expletive. Growing up in an all-male household had done unfortunate damage to a ladylike vocabulary. On New Year's Eve she'd made a resolution to give up cursing, but so far, her progress hadn't been stellar.

Sam's last words still rang in her ears. *Do you have any questions?*

Hell, yes, she had questions, one in particular. *Was I so repulsive seven years ago that you couldn't bring yourself to have sex with me when I threw myself at you and acted like a fool?*

The remembered humiliation churned bile in her stomach. Steering with one hand, she rummaged in her purse for an antacid. The intervening days and months had done nothing to blunt the sharpness of the memory....

"Hi, Sam." She was breathless from running downstairs to intercept him before he got in his car. She'd kept a vigil at her bedroom window for the last half hour. Sam and his father had driven separately, because the older man was lingering to play poker with her father and Uncle Victor.

Sam paused, one hand on the top of the car, the other holding a set of keys. "What's up? I thought you weren't feeling well." His slow drawl and lazy hazel-eyed smile took her breath away.

She bit her lip, legs trembling. She'd feigned a headache to get out of dinner. Sitting across the table from Sam would have been torture, because she dared not let her daddy see how much in love she was. Vincent Wolff was very protective of his baby daughter. She lifted her chin, reaching for calm. "Actually, I had some work to do. I'm graduating from college in a few weeks. And I'll start my master's program. Interior design," she added, hoping he would be impressed. She felt like an adult for the first time in her life, with a level playing field, and the resultant adrenaline gave her confidence.

Sam jingled his keys. "Oh." The look on his face wasn't encouraging. If anything he was eager to get on his way. At almost thirty, Sam Ely was in his prime, and just about the hottest thing Annalise had ever seen.

She moved three steps closer. "I thought you might like to take me out to dinner sometime," she said.

The look on his face—as if he'd been poleaxed—was not flattering.

Desperation lent wings to her feet. She moved forward with determination, went up on tiptoe to wrap her arms around his neck and kissed him square on the mouth. His arms went around her reflexively, but his entire body stiffened. "Um, Annalise..."

She scattered kisses from his nose to his chin to his tanned neck revealed by an open-collared dress shirt. "I know you've been waiting for me to grow up," she whispered. "Please tell me you want me. I know you do."

His burgeoning erection gave truth to her words. But at twenty-one, more naive than most, she didn't fully grasp the difference between male reflex and a more romantic motive.

After one heartfelt moment when it seemed as if Sam might return her kiss, he set her away firmly, holding out a hand when she would have embraced him again. "No, Annalise. I think of you as a sister."

Confusion brought her up short. His body had responded...unmistakably. "I think I'm in love with you, Sam," she cried.

He winced. He actually winced. And her heart turned to ashes.

The kindness in his gaze scorched her with humiliation. "You're barely an adult, honey. And I'm years too old for you. I'm flattered. You're an amazing young woman. But both of our dads would string me up if I tried anything with you... And besides..."

He had said enough. Annalise didn't want to hear any more. She was mute with misery.

"Besides," he said slowly, "most guys like to do the chasing. You might want to think about that. I know you've grown up without a mother to teach you these things, but men like gentle, feminine women. Soft, self-effacing. I guess it's the whole caveman thing." He brushed her cheek with the back of his hand. "You're beautiful, Annalise. You don't need to try so hard...."

The front of the car hit a larger-than-normal pothole, and Annalise was jerked back to the present, clutching the steering wheel as she slowed to a crawl. Please, God, let Sam Ely's visit be short. She would listen politely, take notes and bid him a civil goodbye. Then she could get to work.

If she ignored the debacle from the past, surely he would have the decency to do so as well.

As she rounded one last bend in the road and came in sight of the cluster of buildings that comprised Sycamore Farm, she saw a lone, immediately recognizable figure standing on the front porch despite the frigid temperatures. Her heart beat a sluggish rhythm as she put the car in Park and got out.

She was a grown woman, well-traveled. Sophisticated. Sexually experienced to some degree. She had done everything in her power to forget her first love, to deny how much Sam's rejection had wounded her tender heart. Sam Ely was just a man like any other. For thirty-six hours, forty-eight at the most, she would impress him with her calm competence and her utter lack of interest in his sexy smile and masculine charms. By the time he left, all he would remember about Annalise Wolff was that she was damned good at her job.

He lifted a hand in greeting, the habitual smile nowhere in evidence.

Annalise opened her mouth to say hello. But in an instant that felt like the most dreadful slow-motion replay, disaster struck. Her heel hit a patch of ice in the driveway, her feet flew out from under her and she fell flat on her back. Hard.

When she opened her eyes with a groan, Sam Ely's big body crouched over hers as his hands ran lightly over her limbs checking for damage. Gently he lifted her head and felt for a knot.

Annalise shivered inside her warm down coat, but it had nothing to do with the snow flurries swirling around them. All he had to do was touch her and she was that young, desperate woman again.

He brushed her cheek with the back of his hand. "Are you hurt?"

Sam winnowed his fingers through silky black hair that clung to his fingers with static from the cold air. "Say something, damn it. Are you okay?"

Annalise's glare could have melted a snowman at ten paces. She struggled to sit up. "I'm fine," she said shortly. "Quit pawing me."

Though her words were clipped and showed her annoyance, beneath his touch she was warm and soft and womanly. Resisting the urge to touch the curve of her breast, Sam scooped her into his arms and stood, mentally counting to ten. He'd promised himself he wouldn't let her push his buttons. But she was so aggravating, his blood pressure went up immediately whenever they got within sight of each other. Not that such a reaction was anything new. As a friend of the Wolff family, he inevitably ran into her from time to time. Neither of them ever managed more than bare civility.

The animosity was his fault, no doubt. But it wouldn't hurt her to let go of something that happened over half a dozen years ago. Thankfully, she didn't squirm too much. She was a tall woman, and if he slipped on the ice, they'd both go down.

On the porch, he reached with one hand to open the door and stepped inside, ruefully aware that the house held a distinct chill. He sighed. "The heat and air guys will be here in a couple of days to overhaul the vents and put in new units. In the meantime, I hope you've got plenty of warm clothes. The old system is cantankerous."

"Probably learned it from you," Annalise muttered beneath her breath.

He knew she meant for him to hear.

In the kitchen, he lowered her into a chair. A cheery fire crackled in the fireplace, and his grandmother's collection of Fiestaware in the china cabinet brightened the room.

He knelt in front of her. "Tell me the truth. Are you hurt?"

Big eyes stared back at him. And for an instant, he thought her bottom lip might have quivered. But if there had been even a moment of vulnerability, it was gone.

"No," she said bluntly. "I'm fine." She stripped out of her coat, revealing a thin silky blouse in a shade of blue that matched her eyes, and black linen trousers with a knife pleat. "But I'd kill for a cup of coffee."

For a long second, Sam stayed at her feet. She could have stepped off the runway and come straight to him. Vincent Wolff had kept his baby girl locked up like a nun for much of her life, but probably out of guilt, he had indulged her passion for pretty clothes.

Sam sighed. "Don't try to stand up yet. I'll brew a pot." In moments, the aroma of coffee permeated the air. Annalise hadn't moved from the chair where he put her. But she was pointedly ignoring him, smart phone in hand as she scrolled through messages.

He found a china cup, filled it with hot, fragrant liquid and set it on a saucer at her elbow, along with a tiny pitcher of cream and the sugar bowl. He smothered a grin as she frowned at the add-ons and instead put the cup to her berry-colored lips and drained half of it, black and straight, the same way Sam liked it.

He turned a chair around and straddled it, facing her across the table. "How's your dad?"

She paused, the cup halfway to her mouth. "Fine." Her suspicious gaze scanned his face as if searching for a secret agenda.

"And your uncle Vic?"

Annalise set down the cup. "Also fine."

"Lots of weddings in your family in the last year."

Her face softened. "Yes. It's been wonderful. Gracie, Olivia, Ariel, Gillian… I finally have sisters."

"Your family deserves happiness more than any set of people I know. I'm glad the past is behind you." When Annalise was a toddler, her mother and aunt had been kidnapped and murdered. It was a blow that had marked them all, and it had taken years for them to truly recover.

Annalise's eyebrows lifted, a glint of defiance in her expression. "Thank God for that." She laughed, but there was little humor in the sound. And the sideways glance she shot him said louder than any words that a certain moment in their past was definitely *not* forgotten.

He reached across the table and took her hand in his, stroking the back of it, feeling the smooth skin, the delicate bones. "Give me a break, Annalise. We can't work together if we don't hash this out. I'll admit I could have handled things better back then. But I'd known you since you were in kindergarten. And you were still a kid as far as I was concerned."

She jerked her hand away. "I don't know what you're talking about."

Her scowl would have deterred most men. But Sam was tired of being treated like the Ebenezer Scrooge of the romance world. "Your father would have neutered me."

"You said I was like a sister to you."

"Damn it." His clumsy lie was going to haunt him.

"Clearly, I didn't mean that. I was trying to escape with some grace."

"So you were a lily-livered coward. Is that what you're telling me?"

This time he had to count to fifty. Standing abruptly, he tried not to notice the plump curve of her bottom lip or the way dark lashes made feathered crescents on her cheeks when she looked down at her cup.

"Yes," he said, conceding defeat. If she wanted to hold a grudge, there wasn't a damn thing he could do about it. "I was a coward."

His admission seemed to take the wind out of her sails. "Whatever." She sniffed and crossed her legs, picking at a spot of lint on the cuff of one pant leg.

As a comeback, it lacked a certain vocabularic grace, but he was willing to let it slide. "Why don't I show you your room?" he said, trying to live up to Gram's notion of hospitality. "I'll get your bags. Relax and make sure you didn't do any permanent damage."

Her small, wry grin disarmed him. "My butt bone is probably bruised, but I'll live."

Seeing her smile in his presence was such a novelty, he was momentarily stunned. He swallowed. "I'm glad."

Unable to come up with any response more scintillating than that, he turned and executed what might be considered a hasty retreat, striding down the hallway toward the front of the house in order to give himself time to regain his footing. If Annalise Wolff was going to start smiling at him, all bets were off.

He flung open the front door and stopped dead. A string of heartfelt curses brought his lovely guest running. "What is it? What's wrong?"

They stood shoulder-to-shoulder gazing out into a world

of swirling snow. Already Annalise's tire tracks were being erased. And her car was coated in white.

She punched his arm. "Did you know this was going to happen? Why didn't you tell me not to come?"

His eyebrows reached his hairline. "I've been a little busy, damn it. Did *you* even bother to look at a forecast?"

"This is your fault!" They shouted in unison, with two identical expressions of dismay and disbelief.

Sam closed the door and leaned back, his arms folded across his chest. "I can't tell for sure without checking The Weather Channel, but having spent a lot of years in Virginia, I'd say we're in for a big one."

"I'm sure it's not going to be more than a few inches." The unflappable Annalise Wolff was definitely rattled. A pulse beat visibly in the side of her swanlike neck.

The urge to make an inappropriate sexual comment was strong, but he squelched it. "You seem upset," he said mildly.

It was her turn to do the eyebrow thing. "Seriously? Aren't you the man who doesn't leave the office until nine most nights? You could be stuck here. For hours…maybe days…" Her voice ended on a high squeak.

Oddly, the more she freaked, the greater his sense of amusement. "Don't worry, Annalise. At least we have each other."

Two

Glaring, she thrust out her chin and fisted her hands. "I absolutely will not be locked up in this house with you. No way, no how."

He shrugged. "I promised Gram I'd stay the weekend and get you oriented. But if you're worried about being stuck and alone with me, we can leave right now. She'll be really disappointed...."

He was goading her, and not even trying to hide it. Frustration knotted her belly, even as her recalcitrant imagination conjured up images of the two of them entwined beneath one of Gram's handmade quilts. "I'm not worried about myself. You're the one who needs to get back to work."

"What do you propose we do? I drove the Porsche. You're in a Miata. If we stay here any length of time, neither of us has a prayer of making it back out to the interstate."

His expression was veiled, unreadable. Was this some kind of game where Sam waited to see if she would cry uncle? She wouldn't give him the satisfaction.

"Fine," she said abruptly. "The weather doesn't bother me. But I'd like my bags now, if you don't mind. So I can get settled in." She handed him her keys.

She was pretty sure his jaw dropped a millimeter. Clearly he thought she'd go running back to the city. But Annalise Wolff never backed down from a challenge.

He scowled. "Are you sure about this, Princess? If the power goes out, we'll be roughing it."

Annalise gulped inwardly. Her idea of rustic was not staying on the concierge floor at the Four Seasons. "I'm sure there's a generator…right?"

"Of course. But it won't run forever. Did you even bring any warm clothes besides your coat?" His gaze felt like a caress as he did a visual inventory of her silk blouse and thin slacks.

"I have everything I need. Do you want me to *help* you retrieve the suitcases?"

Her snarky question deepened his frown. "I think I can manage."

She watched through the window and grinned as Sam opened the trunk and did a double take. Hiding her smile, she stayed out of the way while he made three trips in a row, grousing audibly at the mounting pile of luggage.

When he was finally finished, he closed the door behind him and locked it, looking for all the world like a sexy abominable snowman. He shrugged out of his thick jacket and ran a hand through his hair, sending droplets of water flying as melting snowflakes dampened the floor.

Annalise leaned against the wall, trying not to go weak in the knees when his muscles flexed beneath the fabric

of a thermal weave shirt in a deep rust color that comple-
mented his eyes. "Thank you."

He tossed the wet jacket over the back of a chair. "Does
the term *high maintenance* mean anything to you?"

She shrugged. "I plan to be here for several weeks.
Am I supposed to write you a check for excess baggage?"

He stared at her, a long, intense clashing of gazes that
was unmistakably sexual. "You have a smart mouth."

"You have an arrogant attitude."

The ruddy tinge that colored his cheekbones gave her
more satisfaction than it should have. "What's in all those
bags?" he asked, his stance combative.

"Books, laptop, snacks, lingerie…" She gestured toward the pieces of her Louis Vuitton matched set. Uncle
Victor had given it to her as a graduation present. She was
spoiled, she freely admitted it. But that didn't give the insufferable Sam Ely a right to criticize.

"Snacks?" He leaned against the opposite wall, adopt-
ing a pose that mirrored hers. Barely three feet separated
them, and although the foyer was definitely chilly after
Sam had been in and out the door several times, Annalise
was not cold at all.

"I have a weakness for chocolate. So sue me. The stuff
I picked up in Lucerne after Christmas is better than sex."

"Then you've been having the wrong kind of sex."

This time it was her jaw that dropped. Her thighs tightened, and she was pretty sure her nipples were playing
peek-a-boo through the silk of her blouse…though she
wasn't about to check. Surreptitiously, she lifted her folded
arms. "Is flirtation your default setting? Or do you really
expect me to argue the point?"

"You're right," he said smoothly, his voice slow as
syrup. "That was an inappropriate remark between col-
leagues."

"I'm not your colleague," she shot back. "I work for your grandparents."

Sam straightened and closed the distance between them. "You have to forgive me for the past, Annalise. Otherwise we're going to be at each other's throats forever."

She looked at the tanned skin of his jaw and below… saw the way warm, masculine flesh disappeared into the neckline of his henley shirt, revealing a faint dusting of hair where the top two buttons gaped open. Her heart thudded in her chest and her palms were damp.

Licking her lips, she looked past him to the antique grandfather clock that held a place of honor flanking the foot of a curved staircase. "I'm surprised you haven't ever found that paragon of womanhood you described to me. You know, all meek and quiet and docile." Saying the words aloud revived the awful memory of that evening. Her chest hurt.

She heard him curse and felt big, warm hands settle on her shoulders. "Look at me, Princess. I'm sorry. All that crap I said to you that day was just that. I was babbling. Trying to get myself out of a sticky situation. Yes, I was attracted to you. But you had a crush, that's all. That guff I spouted about waiting for a man to make the first move… well, I guess I wanted to make sure you'd never try that stunt again. I didn't want you to end up hurt because some jerk took you up on your offer and then dumped you."

His breath was warm on her face. She dared not look into his eyes. She felt far too fragile, and that really pissed her off, because Annalise Wolff was *not* fragile. She'd grown up in a monster of a house with two brothers, three male cousins, an uncle and a father. Any *girly* ways had been hammered out of her at a young age.

She could climb trees, play football, talk cars and quote

sports statistics with the best of them. And if the need arose, she knew how to fell a man with one quick move.

What she hadn't quite mastered, though, was how a woman could resist when the man she'd wanted for years was so close you could lift your lips and touch your mouth to his.

With every fiber of her being, she yearned to move against him, rest her head on his shoulder and feel his big masculine arms enfold her. But that was exactly why she couldn't.

She was weak when it came to Sam Ely. Weak and dreadfully predictable. So he was handsome, so what? The fact that he was sexy and Southern and so damned funny and smart shouldn't be an issue.

Any notion she'd ever had of snagging Sam had disappeared when she'd embarrassed herself with a youthful, impassioned declaration that was ill-timed to say the least. Sam might pretend he'd only been letting her down easy, but she had a hunch that in their charged encounter way back then, he had been speaking the truth.

Sam's perfect woman was not Annalise. Not by a long shot.

With a strangled mutter of protest, she eluded his embrace, picked up two small bags and headed toward the kitchen. Refusing to look at him, she raised her voice as she walked away. "I'd like another cup of coffee, and then I'd appreciate it if you would show me my room."

Sam grabbed up most of the rest of the bags and followed her, grinding his teeth in frustration. He'd apologized, damn it. What more could he do? He wasn't about to crawl. Especially since he hadn't done anything wrong. In fact, he ought to get a medal for doing the *right* thing. Annalise was one of the most sensual, beautiful women he had ever known. If he'd been a different kind of man—or not suitably intimidated by his father and hers—he would have said *to hell with it* and taken her up on her offer.

He'd certainly thought about it often enough over the years. But he'd been raised to adhere to a gentlemanly code of conduct, and that code precluded a thirty-year-old man from having sex with one not-quite-mature college graduate who'd been sheltered more than most.

He wasn't the bad guy in this scenario. So why did he get the distinct impression that Annalise Wolff would like to consign him to the devil?

Striding through the kitchen and into the hallway beyond, he tried to avoid looking at her. The scent of her perfume, something light and beguiling, mingled with the smell of coffee.

The bedroom that had been prepared for Annalise was as cold as ice. He rolled his eyes in disgust and opened all the vents. Evidently the housekeeping service his grandmother utilized had missed a few key points about dates.

Annalise startled him when she appeared at his side, her arms wrapped around her waist protectively. "It's like a meat locker in here," she said. "Are you sure the heat's working at all?"

He hefted her large suitcase onto a large cedar-lined chest at the foot of the bed. "For now? Yes. But I'll kick the thermostat up a few notches to be sure. It wouldn't kill you to put on a sweater."

"The cold doesn't seem to be bothering you."

"I have a fast metabolism. And quite a few more pounds of insulation than you do." He paused, uncharacteristically uncertain. Of himself. Of her. "Last chance," he said. "If we leave now, I think we can still make it back to town."

Annalise stared at him, eyes wide. "I've cleared my calendar," she said quietly. "This project deserves my full attention. Even with bad weather, there is a lot I can do to keep the ball rolling. Measuring and sketching alone will keep me occupied for several days. But I understand if you need to go back to Charlottesville."

He couldn't read her expression. Weak late-afternoon light, muted by the snow, filtered in through lace sheers, casting dappled shadows on the hardwood floor. "I can't leave you here alone," he said, not really wanting to. "Anything could happen."

She shrugged, glimmers of something disturbing in her eyes. "I'm more resilient than you think. You're not responsible for me."

He allowed himself to touch her briefly, tucking a stray strand of hair behind her ear. "I promised Gram I'd get you started. There's a lot of info I need to share. So I guess we're staying."

He was shocked that she allowed the fleeting touch without protest. A tiny smile kicked up one corner of her mouth. "I guess we are."

At that moment, the lights flickered. Annalise looked at him with apprehension. "Already?"

"It's probably just the wind at this point. Although, to be honest, the power isn't all that reliable on a good week. And by the way, the plans include undergrounding all the utilities. Not only for occasions like today, but to restore the original look of the place."

"Holy cow, Sam. That will cost a fortune."

Coming from the daughter of one of the wealthiest families in America, her amazement was telling. "Yeah," he said, grinning. "But I'm an architectural purist. What can I say?"

The lights flickered a second time, galvanizing him into action. "I need to go bring in as much firewood as I can. If the power goes out, we'll camp out in the living room."

"That's behind the kitchen, right?"

"Yes. The two rooms share a chimney. Fortunately, that section of the house has already been finished. If you don't mind, how about making us a couple of omelets while I get the wood. If we do lose power, it would be nice to have one last hot meal."

Annalise blanched.

"What's wrong?"

"I'm not handy in the kitchen," she said with a wry, self-deprecating twist of her mouth.

"Nothing fancy," he assured her. "There's lunch meat in the fridge. Just chop up some ham."

She grimaced, and for a split second he witnessed in Annalise a shocking vulnerability he had never seen before. "I'm serious, Sam. I don't cook."

The expression on her face seemed to indicate she was awaiting his derision. And although he was certainly incredulous, he tried to hide his surprise. "I guess that makes sense. Growing up without a mother must have been tough."

"I wanted the chef to teach me. When I was thirteen. But Daddy said it was inappropriate for me to spend time in the kitchen when I could be learning Latin and Greek. He has odd ideas about things like that."

"And in college?"

"I lived in the dorm. Ate in the cafeteria. When I got out on my own, it wasn't an issue. I order a lot of take-out, and when I entertain, I hire a caterer."

He was momentarily speechless.

Annalise lifted her chin. "I know your grandmother is a fabulous cook. And I'm sure your mother is, as well. But if that's what you were expecting, you're out of luck. I planned on eating a lot of cereal and canned tuna while I'm here."

Sam inhaled, feeling as though he was stepping through a minefield. "It's not important, Annalise. You caught me off guard, that's all. I have this impression of you as being Superwoman, and I suppose I thought there was nothing you couldn't do."

Her tense shoulders relaxed. "That's a nice thing to say."

He tugged her hair. "I *can* be nice on occasion. When I'm not continually provoked."

"Is that a jab at me?"

He lifted an eyebrow innocently. "Would I do that?"

They laughed softly in unison, and he felt an imperceptible shift in the parameters that had governed the recent cold war between them.

Annalise waved her hands. "Go get the wood. I'll make some sandwiches. And I do know how to heat soup."

"Well, there you go," he said. "What more do we need?"

He found himself whistling as he carried armload after armload of wood into the house from the pile beside the barn. Something inside him felt charged with anticipation, though if he'd been called on to identify the odd feeling, he wouldn't have been able to pin it down. For the moment, he was content to enjoy the prospect of an evening with a beautiful woman.

If they had to rely on the fireplace for everything, the supply of logs would dwindle rapidly. So he labored until his arms ached and his back protested. When he finally was satisfied that they had enough fuel for the immediate future, he replaced the tarp covering the woodpile and prayed they wouldn't need to revisit it anytime soon.

As he returned to the house, a rush of warm air greeted him along with the sound of Adele's voice filling the hallways at high volume. He found Annalise singing along, oblivious to his entrance as she bent over the kitchen table, arranging two place mats at perfect angles and aligning silverware.

It shouldn't have surprised him to see a high-end iPod dock. Those suitcases had been heavy enough to contain a whole range of electronics.

He waved an arm, hoping to catch her peripheral vision, but she jumped anyway, clutching her chest. "You scared me." She turned the volume down several notches. "Are you ready to eat?"

He was still wearing his jacket, which was now really wet, so he hung it over a chair and put the chair near a vent. Annalise set an opened beer and a bowl of tomato soup in front of him and added a small plate laden with a sad-looking grilled cheese. It wasn't exactly burnt, but she had used too much cheese, and the excess had leaked out the side and turned crispy brown.

She hovered until he took a bite of each offering. Then in silence, she brought her own dishes to the table and sat down. With the heat from the stove, the room was finally warm. Out of the corner of his eye, Sam watched her eat. She had tied her hair back in a thick ponytail, revealing a neck begging to be nibbled by some lucky man.

Sam took a swig of beer, swallowed and set the bottle on the table with a muffled *thunk*. Leaning back in his chair, he stared at her. "So tell me, Annalise. Is there some guy back in Charlottesville who's going to be missing you while you're away?"

She gave him a wary, sideways glance. "I'm not seeing anyone at the moment. I've been slammed at work, and frankly, the last man I went out with was a little too needy. I don't have time for all that romantic crap."

He lifted an eyebrow. "Crap?"

"You know. Texting twenty times a day. Long dinners

and hand-holding in the park. Seriously, the man was a walking Hallmark card."

Sam grinned. "A lot of women like that kind of thing."

Annalise frowned at him. "I don't cook and I'm not into romance. Anything else you want to find fault with?"

"Calm down, Princess. I'm not criticizing. I happen to think you're a fantastically talented person. I was impressed with the way you organized that carnival for the new school in Burton." The Wolff family was in the process of funding and building a brand-new school at the foot of Wolff Mountain so the K-8 students wouldn't have to be bussed so far away.

She narrowed her gaze as if trying to discern sarcasm in his words. "I thought I saw you there."

"I didn't speak to you because you were so busy. Like a general in charge of an army. Everything went smoothly as far as I could see."

She nodded, pleasure lighting her face. "The community wanted to be able to invest in the school project financially. And they did…in a big way. The carnival raised a ton of grassroots money."

"You juggle a lot of balls simultaneously. I've noticed that about you." His office and Annalise's were in the same building in downtown Charlottesville. They rarely crossed paths during the day, but they ran in the same social circles and often attended the same charitable events.

"I like to stay busy," she said. She stood and began taking dirty dishes to the sink. Sam had insisted on installing a dishwasher for his grandmother a long time ago, and had even rigged it so that it was virtually unnoticeable in the period kitchen. Annalise loaded the plates and utensils with brisk, efficient movements.

When she was done, she wiped her hands on a gingham dish towel and leaned back against the counter. "Can we do the tour now? I'm eager to get started."

Sam swallowed hard and wished he hadn't finished his beer. Was she doing it on purpose, or was he simply reading into her words his own sexual agenda. "Fine," he croaked.

Annalise grabbed a pen and notebook from the sideboard—she'd obviously been jotting ideas while he'd labored in the snow. "Where do we begin?"

He sighed inwardly, only now beginning to realize what he'd signed on for. Cabin fever, most definitely. And an unfortunately unrequited dose of healthy lust and attraction.

They walked room to room as Sam talked and Annalise scribbled frantically. Once, peeking over her shoulder, he grinned to see that her handwriting resembled a doctor's… sharp and dark and illegible. Every now and then she'd stop and stare, seeming to be visualizing what might be. She talked to herself beneath her breath as she studied angles and walls and lighting.

After an hour, Sam ushered her back to the living room. Holding a match to the already prepared firewood and tinder, he waved Annalise to one of the two leather armchairs that flanked the fireplace. "We might as well be warm and comfortable while we go over the rest of what Gram wanted me to tell you."

Annalise curled up in the comfy seat and tucked her legs beneath her. "You don't know how exciting it is to have carte blanche with a project like this."

He joined her, yawning as the warmth from the fire caught him unawares. He'd headed to bed after one the night before, and the alarm had been set for six. Even though having to stay at Sycamore Farm longer than he had planned would play havoc with his schedule, at this particular moment, he couldn't find it in his heart to care.

Contentment rolled over him in a wave, and his eyes drifted shut.

Annalise was taken aback to hear her host emit a soft snore. She turned to face him and felt a sharp jab in the vicinity of her heart. His legs were propped on an ottoman, and his hands were tucked behind his head. With his big body outstretched, the shirt he was wearing rode up at his belt line, exposing a tantalizing inch of flat, male abdomen.

Annalise was a tall woman, but Sam was taller still, giving her an odd and incomprehensible sensation of delicate femininity. Which was bizarre to say the least, because although she loved fashion and accessories as much or more than the next woman, she wouldn't characterize herself as feminine in the traditional sense.

She was blunt and bold and often spoke her mind when she'd be better served holding her tongue. Arguing came naturally to her, and even as adults, she and her brothers and cousins could go at it at a moment's notice. Not everyone regarded bickering and merciless teasing as an acceptable pastime, though, and with the advent of new family members, the squabbling had been reduced to more socially acceptable standards.

The testosterone-fueled environment Annalise had grown up in had forced her to develop a thick skin. Regrettably, the only person who had ever really had the ability to pierce it at will was presently sitting a few feet away from her.

She wasn't very good at being still, though the house was certainly peaceful. Inactivity provided too much time for introspection, and Annalise was seldom comfortable with that much self-awareness. She preferred to forge ahead and make up the answers along the way.

Gnawing her lip in indecision, she set her notebook on a side table and quietly stood. Already the fire needed another log. Stealthily, she removed the fire screen, lifted a two-foot piece of oak, kneeled and dropped it carefully onto the flaming embers.

Though she'd never had the opportunity to be a Girl Scout, her brothers had taught her all sorts of skills in the forest. As young children they'd tramped around Wolff Mountain and even invented a club, six members strong. The Wolff Mountain gang.

She paused, fire poker in hand, and felt the sting of tears. Where had this sense of melancholy come from? Was it because, one at a time, each member of the old "gang" seemed to be finding happiness? Healing? Peace?

She was thrilled for her cousins and for her big brother, Devlyn. But where did that leave her and Larkin? Would they always be odd men out?

"Do you see something I don't see?" Sam spoke from behind her, startling her so badly she dropped the poker.

She picked it up, rearranged the logs and replaced the screen. At last, she turned to face Sam. Her feelings were too close to the surface, and she feared saying something stupid. "Just enjoying the blaze," she said lightly.

He sat up, yawning. "Sorry to crash on you like that. It's been a long week."

"Since you quizzed me, I suppose it's okay for me to ask if you have a lady friend who will expect you home tomorrow?"

He leaned forward, elbows on his knees, and ran his hands through his hair. "I'm between relationships at the moment," he said, his voice muffled.

Annalise was well aware that Sam Ely was considered

a "catch." Over the years she had noted the stream of females flowing through his life. Noted and been silently
wounded by it. "What happened to the last one?"

His head lifted and he resumed his earlier position. But
although his body language signaled relaxation, his gaze
was guarded. "We differed on some important issues. Politics. Religion."

"And that was enough to forego sex with Diana Sal-
yers?"

He grinned. "You know a lot about me for someone
who hates my guts."

Annalise sniffed. "You paraded her around all over
Charlottesville. Kind of hard to miss. But I'll admit that I
didn't know it was over. You strike me as being the kind
of guy who could overlook things like that."

He grinned. "Touché. All right. If you must know, I
found out she doesn't want to have kids."

Three

Sam took it as a good sign that Annalise was interested in his love life. Not that he had decided to coax his irascible house guest into bed. But it was nice to know there was some level of emotional involvement, despite her determined antipathy.

He crossed one ankle over the other and rubbed his chest with one hand. Annalise's gaze tracked his every move.

She worried her bottom lip. "You want kids?"

Her incredulity nicked him. "I'm on the wrong side of thirty-five. Is that so strange?"

Instead of sitting down, she paced, her nervous energy palpable. "I didn't peg you for the family type. Didn't your parents divorce?"

He nodded. "When I was nine. Dad worked long hours, so Mother got full custody and took me to Alabama, where she was from."

"Hence the accent."

"Yeah. Alabama was great, but I'd visit Dad several times a year, and then every summer, I came here. To Sycamore Farm. Gram and Pops were security. Roots."

"And this farm will all be yours one day."

"I'm in no hurry. It's so far from town I don't know if I'd ever live here full-time. But weekends and vacations certainly. I'd like my sons and daughters to have the same great experiences I remember."

"Kids...plural? I thought children of divorce ended up cynical loners."

"Do I seem like that kind of guy to you?"

She turned to face him, their gazes locking across the room. For long moments the only sound was the pop and crackle of the fire. "No," she said finally. "But I did assume you were a confirmed bachelor."

"Not at all. In fact, when the right woman comes along, I'll snap her up and hopefully give Gram and Pops some great-grandchildren while they're still young enough to enjoy them."

"Interesting." Annalise walked to the window and tugged aside thick brocade draperies. Darkness had fallen and the glass was too frosted to see anything anyway.

He couldn't read her at the moment. "What about you?" he asked. "Are you going to ride the wave of happily-ever-afters that has overtaken the Wolff family?"

She turned, clearly shocked. "Me? Oh, no. And definitely not kids. It wouldn't be fair."

There was no palatable explanation for the leaden block of disappointment in his stomach. "How so?"

Now she paced behind him, meaning that unless he wanted to stand up and join her, he had no way of studying her expression. He stayed seated and gave her the space she seemed to need.

Her voice was almost wistful. "I've never been around children. At all. You know that none of us were allowed to go to school until we were college-aged."

"You had private tutors, right?"

"Yes. And let me tell you, I had a really hard time making friends when I was an eighteen-year-old college freshman. All I knew was how to relate to guys. Girls were a mystery to me, and sororities, giggling confidences, sexual bragging… All of it baffled me."

"What does any of this have to do with having kids?"

"Let's just say I'm not the nurturing type and leave it at that."

Her answer unsettled him. He felt sure there was more to the story. But they didn't have the kind of relationship where he could drag it out of her. After all, he was lucky to be sharing a house without armed hostilities.

He waved a hand over the back of his chair. "Come sit down. Let me tell you what Gram wants." With the cozy fire and the sense of isolation bred by the storm, the room had become far too intimate.

By the time he retrieved his briefcase from the kitchen and extracted a folder, Annalise was sitting with suspect docility in her chair by the hearth. He'd half expected her to change into jeans and a sweatshirt, but then again, he wasn't sure she owned anything that plebian.

Merely looking at her threatened his peace of mind. She was the kind of beautiful that made a man's heart ache. And other parts of him…well, hell. His body reacted predictably.

Trying to ignore the picture she made, he sat back down, clearing his throat. "How much do you know about the house?"

"Not too much, really. I'm all ears."

She had taken her hair down, and now it floated around

her shoulders, black as sin and just as appealing. As he watched, mouth dry, she curled one strand around her finger and played with it absently. The innocently sensuous motion of her hand mesmerized him.

He dragged his gaze away and stared blindly at the papers in his hand.

"Tell me," she said impatiently. "The more I know, the better I'll be able to recreate the past. Every house has a living memory. My job is to find it here at Sycamore Farm."

"Right." He gathered his thoughts and tried to pretend he was talking to a stranger. "Sycamore Farm dates back to the time of Jefferson and Monticello. Some journals even suggest that one of my long ago ancestors was a friend of the Jeffersons, but that hasn't been proven."

"Still, it's fun to think about. And the two properties are not all that far apart as the crow flies."

"True. At any rate, we lost the land for about twenty-five years late in the nineteenth century, after the Civil War. The house suffered some damage and the family experienced financial reversals. But fortunately an enterprising Ely farmer bought it back about 1900, and it's been in the fold ever since."

"I love to think about that lineage. You're very lucky, Sam."

"Your dad and uncle have begun something similar at Wolff Mountain. I know the Wolff legacy was born in darkness, but think about the years ahead. Especially with all the weddings and babies on the way."

"Only one baby so far, and that's a few months away. Little Cammie was already five when we met her, so having a newborn on the mountain really will be different."

"Don't you think *you'll* want a house up there at some point?"

His question seemed to take her by surprise. "I haven't thought about it."

"Liar."

Her head snapped around so fast it was a wonder she didn't have whiplash. "What does that mean?" Indignant and offended, she glared at him. Ah, that was the Annalise he was accustomed to seeing. "It means that I know you, Princess. You're a decorator. You live for color and lighting and creating beautiful spaces. You can't tell me you haven't daydreamed about your own place on the mountain."

Her eyes darkened. "I have such mixed emotions about Wolff Mountain," she said softly. "Whenever I go there, it brings it all back. Tragedy and family and sadness and home. I'm not sure I want to perpetuate that."

"I could help you design it." He wasn't sure where the words came from. They tumbled from his lips uncensored.

She stared, her eyes huge. "You would?"

"Of course. It would be an honor. I feel like my dad's involvement in creating the castle makes me an honorary Wolff, anyway. And even if you build your own place, you could still live in Charlottesville."

A small smile teased her lips. "I may hold you to that."

"I'm a man of my word."

They looked at each other, Sam itchy and aroused and unused to being locked up in a cozy room with a woman who pushed his buttons so successfully. And God knew what the unpredictable Annalise Wolff was thinking. Probably diabolical ways to smother him in his sleep.

He *would* consider seducing her if he wasn't fairly certain she'd go after his private parts with a butcher knife. *Beware a woman scorned.* The old adage rang in his ears, though he hadn't scorned her in the traditional sense. But any softer feelings she felt for him so long ago were clearly dead and buried.

Annalise wrinkled her nose. "We keep getting side-tracked. Tell me what your grandmother is thinking about colors and fabrics."

He leaned forward, handing her several sheets of paper clipped together. When his fingers brushed hers, he felt an unmistakable burst of heat. "She wrote a lot of stuff out for you to go by. I think she trusts you a great deal. She mostly included things she wants kept the same. Other than that, you can do that magic that you do and make Sycamore Farm a showplace."

As Annalise read through what he had given her, Sam added more logs to the fire and went back out onto the front porch to assess the situation. It wasn't good. They were closing in on twelve inches, with no end in sight. He stood there in his shirt sleeves for a moment, feeling the bitter sting of wind and ice crystals on his face.

The frigid air was almost a relief. His reaction to Annalise Wolff had taken him entirely off guard. The attraction was nothing new. He'd watched her grow from a child into a beautiful, vibrant woman over the years. And even when she had thrown herself at him, he'd been tempted. Really tempted.

But at no time since then had he ever really entertained the idea of pursuing her. First and foremost because she had such a damned big chip on her shoulder about him rejecting her. And then there was the almost inevitable awkwardness if they tried something and it didn't work.

Sam and his dad were welcome visitors at Wolff Castle at least on a monthly basis. What would happen if Sam dated Annalise, slept with her and ended things? The fall-out had the potential to disrupt relationships that were years in the making.

For a brief moment he allowed himself to consider the possibility that he and Annalise might be good together.

Really good. Wedding bells and white dress good. He was ready to settle down, more than ready. His own childhood had been decent, but he had always envied the Wolff kids and their invisible but unmistakable bond.

Sam wanted his own children, whenever they came along, to have siblings, to experience the fun and security of knowing that someone always had your back. The Wolffs had been good to him when he visited with his father over the years. But Sam was older even than Gareth, so he hadn't really been able to assimilate into the pack.

As an adult man, he'd forged lasting friendships with all of them. He was particularly close to Jacob and Devlyn. Annalise was the only real holdout, and apparently in her eyes, Sam would always be to blame for their standoff. He was willing to expend the required energy to win her over, but what then? If a romantic liaison went awry, it would be World War III all over again, only this time with no hope of détente.

Shivering hard, he turned his back on the blizzard and went inside.

By the time Annalise finished reading through all the notes Sam's grandmother had made, Sam still had not returned. She added one more log to the blaze and then went to her room to unpack. The antiques spread throughout the house had been lovingly cared for, and it was heartening to know that many of them would be preserved in the newly renovated house.

After filling the narrow closet and most of the drawers in the dresser and armoire, she folded back the covers and tossed her gown and robe on the bed. The beautiful pieces were silk and not very warm. Perhaps she should have thought through the ramifications of sleeping in a drafty farmhouse in the dead of winter.

As she passed by the mirror with its wavy, slightly mottled glass, she stopped and stared at her reflection. What did Sam see when he looked at her? Was she still the socially awkward, love-stricken young woman to him?

Thinking about that dreadful moment in the past was physically painful. It was more than embarrassment. *That* she could have moved beyond. But the hurt that ran deeper was his criticism. Even as he'd said the words aloud, she had recognized the truth of them. She *was* too pushy, too oblivious to other people's feelings at times.

A more experienced woman would have gauged Sam's disinterest and backed off. But all Annalise had been able to recognize was her own desperate longing for the young teenage boy she had adored as a child. The adolescent boy who had gone on to become a breathtakingly handsome man.

"Are you all settled in? Do you need anything?"

Sam lounged in the doorway, effortlessly charming and charismatic. His head nearly brushed the lintel. All of a sudden, the small, delightful bedroom felt claustrophobic.

Annalise felt panic creep into her throat. What if he could see how much he still affected her? Even worse, what if he thought she was pathetic? Lusting after a man who was no more than a family friend.

She cleared her throat. "I think I'll hit the sack. Good night."

He glanced at his watch. "It's eight-thirty, Annalise."

"Oh." Busted. Had she even brought a book to read? "I don't suppose there's internet?"

He chuckled. "Are you kidding? Gram and Pops are pretty much up with the times, but they flatly refused to get a computer. Even though I begged. It might be a different story now that they're in Florida. We'll see. But you've got your phone…you should be able to check email as long as the storm isn't disrupting tower signals."

He paused, shifted from one foot to another, then gave her a lopsided grin. "There's something I could show you… if you're not too tired. But you'll definitely need a coat or sweater, because it's on the third floor."

She nodded slowly. "Okay." Grabbing up a soft suede jacket, she slipped her arms into the sleeves and scooped her hair out of the collar. "I'm ready."

Sam didn't bother with another layer. Apparently he was made of tougher stuff. She followed him up one set of stairs and then another, pausing at a landing as Sam found a key on his key ring and unlocked a rather short door. Ducking to follow him in, she inhaled the scent of history…dust, old paper and the passage of time.

Sam reached up and pulled the chain to illuminate a single lightbulb suspended from the rafters. The space in which they stood ran half the length of the house. It was bone-chillingly cold, and the storm winds shrieked around the gables of the roof with magnified ferocity.

Annalise shuffled from one foot to the other, arms wrapped around her waist. "This better be good."

The grin Sam cast over his shoulder made her weak in the knees. "Follow me." He led her down one side of the room to a section of the attic that had obviously once been walled in. "I imagine this might have been used as servant quarters years ago." Although segments of the wall were nothing more than exposed two-by-fours or whatever the historical equivalent was, part of a single section was still covered in wallpaper. Really old wallpaper.

Annalise bent forward, trying to get close enough to see in the dim light. "Jiminy Christmas, Sam. Is this original?"

She felt his presence, big and warm, at her shoulder. "Jiminy Christmas?"

Heat washed up her throat. "I made a New Year's resolution to give up cussing."

"Ah." He was so close she could inhale his clean, male scent, so close she could hear him breathe.

Doggedly, she focused her attention on the wall. "Has anyone on the historical renovation team seen this?"

Sam pulled a small flashlight out of his hip pocket and handed it to her. "No. But the plan doesn't call for any changes up here. You're one of the only people I know who would get excited about this."

She shone the small beam of light on the edge of the faded paper. Once upon a time it had probably been a cheery yellow. Now, the scattering of small flowers was barely visible on a field of cream. "There's more under here, isn't there?"

She sensed rather than saw him nod. "I've picked at the frayed part enough to tell that there are at least three more layers beneath this. I think that with an X-Acto knife we might be able to extract the various pieces so that you could look at them."

"This is so damn cool!" She clapped her hand over her mouth and heard Sam laugh. "Is there or was there anything like this downstairs?" she asked, hoping to distract him from her failings.

"If so, it's long gone. You'll find Sheetrock and more modern building supplies. But I know Gram would be thrilled if you were able to find a paper similar to one of these and use it in at least one room…just to tie the past to the future."

"I'd love to try. But why do you think they would have gone to the trouble to use wallpaper up here if it was for servants?"

"My guess is that the paper was a way to keep wind

out. Back then, before roofing was really well done, I'm sure this area of the house was almost like living outside."

"Hmmm…" Her brain raced even as she absorbed the fact that she and Sam stood shoulder-to-shoulder. He seemed to be almost deliberately crowding her personal space.

Her jacket was warm, and with Sam in touchable distance her blood was pumping. The cold didn't even register at the moment. Nevertheless, she feigned a shiver. "I'll come back up here one day when I can see better."

"I could show you more treasures. Disintegrating silk dresses with bustles and button-up shoes. Old army uniforms. Collections of sabers and muskets. Even Gram's wedding dress."

She faced him, wondering what he would do if she went up on tiptoe and kissed him. "It will keep, won't it? I think I'm ready for bed. It's been a long day." She handed over the flashlight, and he tucked it in his pocket. But neither of them moved.

"Annalise, I…"

She'd never heard Sam Ely sound unsure of himself. And the scowl that etched tight planes on his face wasn't encouraging.

Sexual tension arced and crackled between them. If it had been any other man, any other situation, Annalise would have initiated a kiss. But the specter of Sam from the past held her back. *Guys like to do the chasing.*

Confused, embarrassed and angry with herself for acting like a 1950s debutante, she turned abruptly. "I'm done here."

She had taken three steps in the direction of the door when the lights went out. Her momentum carried her forward, and she tripped over something on the floor and stumbled to her knees. "Ouch, damn it." Pain shot up her leg to her hip, and her big toe throbbed.

"Hold still. Don't move." Sam rustled behind her, and muttered beneath his breath when something fell to the floor with a loud *thunk*.

"What was that?"

"I dropped the stupid flashlight." He crouched beside her, reaching out in the darkness. "Are you still in one piece?"

"Bruised but functional."

"Let me help you up." His arms went around her and they both froze.

"Sam," she said, her voice unsteady. "That's my boob you're holding."

He released her like a man backing away from a poisonous snake. "Sorry."

She found his hand with hers. "Pull." Gradually, wincing as her knee protested, she made it upright. "Okay then. I can walk."

"Not without me, you can't. Hold on to the back of my belt and I'll get us to the door."

"Are we going to look for the flashlight?"

"No. Who knows how far it rolled, and I have several more downstairs."

She had to touch his waist, brush his hip, to find her way around to his back. And she was pretty sure he inhaled sharply when her fingers curled around his belt and brushed his spine. His skin was smooth and hot to the touch.

A step at a time they made their way through the stygian gloom. What had been a short distance before now became an obstacle course. Suddenly, Annalise yelped and pressed into Sam, wrapping her arms around his waist.

She felt him tense. "What's the matter?"

"Something ran across my foot."

"Probably just a mouse."

"*Just* a mouse?"

"I know you've had the occasional rodent in Wolff Castle."

"I didn't play footsie with them," she complained, shuddering. With all the lights out, who knows how many creatures would come out to play?

"The Annalise Wolff I used to know wasn't afraid of anything. Your brothers and cousins dared you to try all sorts of ridiculous stunts, and you took the bait every time, determined to prove you were as good as they were."

"Well, I've matured since then."

He cursed as they both staggered around some kind of chest. "Too bad…I kind of liked that crazy girl."

Annalise didn't have an answer for that. Was he trying to tell her something, or was this chitchat designed to distract her from the fact that with the electricity out, this old house was going to chill rapidly?

At last Sam located the door, which was rather anticlimactic, because as soon as they stepped through it, they were no better off than they were before. Now they faced two steep flights of stairs.

He ran his palm down her arm, ultimately linking their fingers. "Stay close. I'll follow the stair rail, and you hang on to me."

Annalise wasn't about to argue. Her heart was dancing to some kind of ragged staccato beat and her lung capacity had shrunk to nothing. Not even to herself would she admit that holding hands with Sam Ely rocked her world.

"Works for me," she said, trying to sound matter-of-fact. His grip was firm and warm, unbelievably so, since her own smaller hand was icy.

It was a clumsy sort of ballet, but it worked, albeit

slowly. At the second-floor landing they stopped to catch their breath. Sam squeezed her fingers. "You doing okay, Princess? I know you didn't sign on for this."

It seemed as if he surrounded her, all hard muscle, broad chest and gravelly voice.

She swallowed, her throat dry as the dust that danced in drafts beneath the roof. "Not to worry. I may not have been a Girl Scout, but I can handle you and a dark house."

Four

Sam was disoriented, and it had more to do with having Annalise Wolff clinging to him than it did with the lack of electricity. He was getting definite mixed signals. One wrong move on his part could be disastrous.

Right now, she was silent, seemingly docile. Perhaps regretting her last boastful retort. He was pretty sure she hadn't meant for it to come out sounding like sexual innuendo.

He sighed inwardly. Rarely did he find himself wandering in the dark when it came to a woman, and now he was in the position of doing so both literally and metaphorically. Keeping his voice neutral, he tugged on her hand. "Ready to keep going?"

He felt her nod. "Yes. Won't there at least be some firelight from the kitchen and living room?"

Stepping gingerly down one step and then another, he

led her behind him. "As long as the embers haven't burned too low."

Moments later they made it to the hallway.

She exhaled. "Well, we didn't break a leg. That's something."

He could tell that Annalise was ready to escape into her bedroom and call it a night, but he kept a firm grip on her hand. "We need a snack. Dinner was a long time ago. Can I interest you in a s'more?"

"Served by a roaring fire? Sure."

He steered her to her earlier seat. "Sit here and don't move. We're surrounded by lethal furniture. I'll go find the flashlights." He wasn't gone more than two minutes. Grabbing what he needed out of the kitchen, he returned to find Annalise stoking the fire. The roaring flames danced and crackled, spreading a semicircle of light and warmth.

"What part of *sit still* don't you understand?" Joining her in front of the hearth, he laid two sets of graham crackers and chocolate bars on the mantel and then ripped open a bag of marshmallows. Threading one onto a wire coat hanger, he handed it to her.

She stared at it, a small smile on her face. "I love mine burnt to a nice dark brown."

"Says the woman who doesn't cook. The trick is to get it hot and gooey without involving carcinogens."

"Oh, pooh." She crouched and thrust her marshmallow deep into the flames. "Live a little, Sam."

Again, that odd frisson of awareness. He wasn't convinced she knew how her sharp-edged repartee was affecting him. But maybe he was naive. Perhaps Annalise Wolff was planning sexual revenge and knew exactly what she was doing. He couldn't imagine what that would look like or what her goal could be other than to torment him, but already his body betrayed him.

He wanted to strip her naked and take her there on the rag rug, uncaring that snow drifted deeper and deeper against the windows or that he and Annalise were like oil and water.

Here—and now—he wanted her.

Before he could formulate a suitably masculine retort, Annalise stood abruptly. "Hold this, please."

When he took the coat hanger from her without complaint, she stripped off her jacket and fanned her face. "I think I'm the one melting, not the marshmallow."

Good Lord. That damned silk blouse clung to her arms and breasts with static electricity, outlining pert nipples that riveted his attention even through the evidence of a lacy bra.

He turned away, shocked by how quickly his arousal segued from piqued interest to heavy, molten lust. "Here. Take it back," he croaked. "I'm not going to be responsible for cooking this. Do it your own way."

"Thank you," she mocked. "I will."

As he rotated his coat hanger in precise increments, Annalise laughed when her marshmallow burst into flame. The sound of that husky, sensual chuckle did to his insides what the hot fire had done to puffy white sugar. He was ablaze suddenly, so hungry for her he was actually stunned.

"Blow it out," he said. "Before you ruin it completely."

She waited two clicks—two interminable seconds—and then she did as he commanded. "You just can't stand not to boss me around. That doesn't bode well for our collaboration."

"It's not a collaboration," he insisted. "You're in charge."

She snorted. "Yeah right." Reaching for the rest of her s'more sandwich, she trapped the marshmallow between the other layers and extracted the coat hanger.

"You're gonna burn your tongue."

Annalise bit into her messy s'more and groaned. "Wow. These are amazing. Great idea, Sam."

He pulled his perfectly browned marshmallow from the fire and made his own s'more. He was hungry. And the melted chocolate and marshmallow smelled wonderful. But he couldn't look away from Annalise. Firelight painted her classic features with warm, golden hues. Her mouth was sticky with sugar and chocolate.

"You've got some on your chin," he said gruffly.

She reached up, eyes dancing with laughter, and rubbed a spot. "Did I get it?"

"No." *Lick it. Kiss it. Make her want you like you want her.* The little devil on his shoulder had gotten him into trouble more than once. But something stopped him. A dead certainty that this time he didn't want to screw things up with Annalise Wolff.

He took his thumb and rubbed it across the side of her chin. "There," he said, throat dry. "All clean."

The smile disappeared from her face, and her eyes widened, something unidentifiable flickering in the depths of her wary gaze. "Thank you."

They finished eating in silence. Watching her lick her fingers nearly did him in. "I'll get you a flashlight," he said gruffly. "And there are extra covers in the chest at the foot of your bed."

"Don't worry about me," she said. "Once I burrow under a pile of quilts, I won't come out till morning."

"I'll be sleeping upstairs. Is it going to bother you to be down here alone? If you're worried, I can camp out on the sofa."

Even in the shadowy room he could see her roll her eyes. "Get serious, Sam. Do I strike you as the nervous type? I'll be fine. Besides, there's no way you could stretch out on that couch. You're far too big."

Again, a seemingly innocuous comment with an undercurrent of sexual nuance. "Your choice," he said. And wasn't that the problem? Given their past, for him to make a move on her was risky in the extreme. But in light of his long-ago sins, the likelihood of Annalise Wolff pursuing him a second time was almost nonexistent.

Where did that leave a man who was breathless with wanting and aching for one woman in particular?

"So when do you break out the generator? I assume there is one."

"Yes. But we don't know how long we're going to be stuck, so I suggest we use it sparingly. If you can make it through this one night, we'll power it up tomorrow to cook a decent meal and take showers, anything else we need to do."

"Makes sense."

Annalise was not a whiner. Thank God for that. As soon as he gave her a flashlight, she disappeared with a muttered *good-night*. It didn't escape his notice that when she left him, the novelty and fun of being snowed in vanished. Now he was cold and grumpy and hard…with a long, unpleasant night ahead.

He made sure both of the fires were banked and the screens in place. After clearing up the mess from their bedtime snack, he found his way upstairs. The air was so cold he almost expected to inhale ice crystals.

His bedroom, the one he stayed in when he visited his grandparents, was furnished with more modern items, including a king-size bed. Since he was well over six feet tall, he appreciated the concession. Sleeping in a narrow antique bed had never interested him. At least not until tonight. If Annalise had invited him to share hers, he'd have been more than willing.

In the modern, newly renovated bathroom he made quick work of washing up in the dark. A shower at the moment was out of the question. It might have done him some good considering the fact that he had been semi-aroused for the last three hours. But the house was just too damn cold.

He never used pajamas, and tonight, he bitterly regretted that decision. The sheets felt damp, even though he knew they were not. Huddling into the covers, he tried not to think about what it would be like to have a warm, feminine body curled against his.

Exhaustion claimed him quickly, but he slept in fits and starts. Dreams plagued him. The unrelenting winds rattled the windows and howled around the eaves. At one point he sat up and looked at his phone. Hell, it was only 2:00 a.m.

The cold seeped into his bones. He started worrying about Annalise. But her room was just off the living room and no doubt had benefited to some extent from the fire. And he couldn't imagine that she slept naked. As much as she enjoyed pretty clothes, she probably packed all kinds of sleepwear.

In lieu of counting sheep, he began picturing her in various sexy outfits. Teddies. Football jerseys and knit shorts. Elegant negligees. Camis and thongs.

His imagination was regrettably thorough. Cursing roughly, he cupped his hand around his aching shaft. He didn't want to find relief in that way. He didn't want to be alone.

Another half hour passed. He was more awake than ever. Surely a warm room was preferable to this misery, even if he did have to sleep with his legs hanging off the end of the couch.

Climbing out of bed, he winced when his bare feet met the cold wooden floor. He dressed rapidly in a pair of old, soft jeans and a flannel shirt that he wore when he did chores in the barn. Dragging two pairs of socks over his feet, he grabbed his flashlight and crept downstairs.

Sadly, Annalise's door was firmly closed.

He walked quietly into the living room and shut himself in, away from temptation. His nose detected the faint scent of burnt marshmallow in the air. He had to smile, despite his discomfort. Annalise was never boring.

Crouching on the hearth, he shoved twisted newspaper into the midst of the glowing coals. When a tiny flame erupted, he fed it, using an old-fashioned bellows to encourage the sparks. He thought ruefully of the high-tech gas fireplace in his condo overlooking Charlottesville and the mountains beyond. His home was exactly that— a home. He entertained there, relaxed there, and sometimes when the mood struck him, even worked from home.

He had bought an industrial loft five years ago, torn out almost every wall and redesigned the space exactly the way he wanted it. The resultant living areas were open and roomy, but comfortable and welcoming at the end of a long day.

Like his father, he had a hard time turning down new clients. He loved what he did, and it was both challenging and personally satisfying to give families and small businesses a manifestation of the dreams they carried in their hearts and minds.

Seeing a new structure come to life on paper was a creative and artistic endeavor. Making the reality happen involved hard work and occasionally a dose of informal mediation when a husband wanted a man-cave and his wife a mini-gym.

Sam prided himself on being able to give them both.

He was a problem solver. Unfortunately, one of his biggest problems at the moment lay only a few feet away, fast asleep. It was anyone's guess as to whether or not he and Annalise would reach an understanding…or perhaps even something far more interesting.

Adding a final log to the fire, he rose to his feet, stretched and turned to survey the sofa. It sat farther back in the room at right angles to the fireplace. It wasn't much of a decision to choose the leather chair and ottoman he had occupied earlier. Pulling them even closer to the fire, he grabbed an afghan and prepared to stretch out for what remained of the night.

Before he could sit down, he realized he hadn't replaced the fire screen. He picked up the unwieldy antique and moved it into position, but in doing so, knocked over the bellows, which in turn tumbled into a large brass urn, crashing it to the floor.

He froze, hearing the sound echo through the house. Was Annalise a light sleeper? Ten seconds passed…fifteen…the silence told him he was home free.

With a groan of exhaustion, he settled into the chair, pulled the cover to his chin and crossed his ankles. The position was semicomfortable. His eyelids grew heavy, and he watched the wildly dancing flames through his lashes, remembering bonfires from when he was a kid.

He was almost asleep when a female voice, laden with irritation, spoke not two feet behind him. "Good Lord. What are you doing down here? You scared me to death. I thought an animal had gotten into the house."

Closing his eyes and counting to ten, he tried to assess the situation rationally. But even the sound of her voice turned him on, despite the fact that the tone was more angry than amorous. "I couldn't sleep. That upstairs bedroom is like a morgue during an ice storm."

"Tell me about it."

"I thought you weren't afraid to stay down here by yourself," he taunted. *That's right, Sam. Provoke the beast. Sarcasm will make things better.* He tossed aside the light blanket and stood, only to feel a blow to the chest when he saw her for the first time. In one hand, she brandished a can of pepper spray. With the other she clutched the flashlight he had given her. But what was in between... sweet heaven...

Crimson silk edged in expensive black lace slid sinuously over her body, whispering seduction with every move she made. He scrubbed the heels of his hands over his eyes and yawned, giving himself a chance to swallow the lump of emotion in his throat. Annalise Wolff had grown into an exquisitely beautiful woman.

The stunning view was imprinted on his brain. The gown plunged in front, revealing the swells of soft, creamy-skinned breasts. The thin robe that covered the gown was long-sleeved, but hung open, hiding little. On her feet Annalise wore black satin slippers embroidered in red and gold thread with tiny birds and flowers.

The fact that he could describe her footwear in so much detail only spoke to how hard he was trying not to stare at her chest.

When he finally looked up, she was eyeing him curiously.

"What?" he asked, wondering if he had soot on his face.

She shrugged. "I'm accustomed to seeing you in a suit and tie, or even a tux. This casual 'cowboy' look takes some getting used to."

He might be half-asleep, but he knew interest when he saw it in a woman's eyes. Rounding the chair, he took the flashlight and spray from her hands and set them on a bookcase. "Do you often have animals in the house at

Wolff Mountain?" He was standing so close to her he could see the faint throb of a pulse in her neck.

She flushed. "We've had the occasional bear."

"Inside?"

"I've read stories about such things."

"And you were going to attack a bear with your bare hands? Surely you know that pepper spray makes them more aggressive...and that flashlight is not big enough to do any harm."

"You're insufferable. Has anyone ever told you that?"

Without her habitual three-inch heels, she seemed much smaller...fragile even. And in the middle of the night, with her defenses down, infinitely more approachable. "*You* have," he said, studying her moist, curved lips. "A dozen times. At least when you were willing to speak to me."

He put his hands on her shoulders, waiting to see if she would react, perhaps slap him.

She was heavy-eyed and sleep-rumpled, her thick, shiny black hair hanging almost to her waist. "What are you doing?" she questioned in a husky voice that made him imagine long Saturday mornings in bed.

The room was full of shadows, the hour late. He was tired of reliving the past with this woman. Time to start something new. "I'm going to kiss you."

Her eyes flared wide, but other than that, she made no response. He still had no guarantee this wasn't entrapment. Perhaps he ought to have worn some kind of protective clothing. He knew from hearing Vincent brag that Annalise had a black belt in karate and was fully capable of taking Sam down.

He wanted her to make the first move, craved it, really. But that wasn't going to happen. Not with the painful memory of the last time they both stood on this precipice echoing between them.

Bending his head, he nibbled her neck, inhaling a scent that was so intrinsically *her*. Feminine, yes, but strong, unforgettable. His hands slid down her arms, around her waist, over her butt. She was firm and fit, her soft resilient skin underlain with sleek sexy muscles.

Never had he felt or seen her so still, so submissive. And it worried him. Pulling back, he searched her face. "Touch me," he begged. "Please."

As if his words had broken some kind of weird spell, she moved. With a little murmur that might have signaled any one of a number of emotions, she wrapped one arm around his neck and found his mouth with hers. With her free hand she shoved up the tail of his shirt and stroked his chest. Her touch burned him. It had been years since their first and only kiss, but he remembered the taste of her as if it had been only yesterday.

His tongue plundered the sweet recesses of her mouth, tangling with hers. Gasps and moans were barely audible over the sound of his heartbeat in his ears.

The erection he was unable to hide pulsed between them, thick and hard and ready. When he ground his hips against her belly, she whimpered. Need built and crashed over him, invisible but inescapable. He slid the robe down her arms and let it drop. Lifting her by her ass, he carried her to the chair beside the fire and held her in his lap, bending her back over his arm to kiss her wildly.

Her hair was a silken waterfall. He grabbed handfuls of it, using the grip to guide her mouth to his. Somewhere, deep inside a single rational thought cell, he acknowledged that this was insanity. But the impossible had happened. Annalise, who would normally as soon hiss at him as speak cordially, was actually passionately, eagerly, returning his kiss.

His hands trembled, moving recklessly all over her body.

A nipped-in waist, delicate collarbone, gently curved stomach. Nipples that begged to be touched, pinched, soothed with a kiss. He left the bodice in place. If he stripped her at this point, it was all over. He lifted the hem of her gown and touched her leg, finding nothing but hot skin.

When he moved halfway up her thigh, Annalise clamped her hand over his, blocking further exploration. "Stop," she said hoarsely.

He did, but it cost him dearly. Every sinew in his body throbbed with the need to take, regardless. "I want you, Princess. God knows, I do."

There was a momentary hesitation as if, even for her, the interruption was agonizing. Without warning she slid from his lap and faced him, arms wrapped around her waist, ebony hair a mad tangle. With the firelight behind her, he could see the outline of her slim legs through the thin fabric of her gown. Tears glittered in her eyes, and her distress strafed him with a thousand knives. Why could he never get this right?

He stood as well, but she held up a hand. "Don't come any closer."

"Talk to me," he begged. "Tell me what you want."

Her eyes were tragic, the blue dulled almost to gray. She began to speak. Stopped. Swallowed hard. It almost seemed as if she were holding herself tightly to keep from shattering into irreparable pieces. "Did you have this in mind when you came here this weekend?" she asked, her voice low and broken.

"No," he muttered, staring past her into the fire for a moment and then returning his gaze to her face. "No," he said more forcefully.

His groin ached, his eyes were gritty with lack of sleep and his breath came in great gulps that did nothing to help him relax.

It was the wrong answer. Somehow he knew that instantly. Grief flashed in her eyes and disappeared, leaving nothing but blank, mute misery in its wake. "I know we're snowed in, Sam, but surely you could go without sex for one night. I won't be your easy lay, your sadly predictable one-night stand."

"That's not what this is, damn it." His gut felt like the time he had suffered an appendicitis attack. "You're special. How can you not know that?"

He took her in his arms again, and this time she didn't protest. But the fevered beauty he'd held moments ago had turned to ice. He kissed her again and again…tender kisses, slow drugging kisses. All he accomplished was making himself miserable.

She fit so perfectly in his arms, it was an absolute miracle. How could she not see it?

His own behavior sickened him. Had he told her the truth, or was his subconscious a devious bastard? Had he jumped at Gram's request in order finally to have Annalise where he wanted her?

God, please let that not be true. If it was, he honestly hadn't planned it.

Shocked by his own uncertainty, he released her and stepped back. "I've been attracted to you for years, Annalise, but the timing is always wrong between us. Maybe I did look forward to being here with you, but is that so terrible? You can barely bring yourself to acknowledge me across a crowded room when we cross paths in Charlottesville. We're here now. Alone. For God knows how long. Won't you give me a chance to regain your trust? Please?"

He saw her lower lip wobble before she steadied it with small, even white teeth. "I came here to work for your Gram and Pops. None of this should have happened."

"But it did," Sam said firmly. "And you were right there with me. So don't pretend with me, Annalise. We both stepped into that fire."

Five

If Annalise had ever been more stricken with mortification, she couldn't remember it. In many ways, the ramifications of this moment with Sam were even worse than what had happened years ago. At least back then he had written her girlish passion off to immaturity.

Now, in one mad instant, she had revealed her deep vulnerability where he was concerned. Not only to him, but also to herself. She'd been pretending for years that she hated Sam Ely. The truth was, she was probably in love with him. She wasn't exactly sure what that emotion was supposed to feel like. Surely not this nauseous sensation of impending doom.

At twenty-one she had known what she wanted and gone after it. Sam had crushed her budding attempt to be a sexually confident woman. Now, here he was. Gorgeous. Hungry. And ready to take advantage of propinquity and auld lang syne.

If she overreacted, she risked letting him see straight into her heart and her soul. Wolffs guarded both those locations zealously. Too much tragedy and heartache in the past to be soft. Too much at stake to voluntarily open up to the possibility of pain and loss.

So she had a choice. She could play this cool, run the show. Or she could let Sam break her heart. Given that pairing, it was really no contest.

Gathering the shreds of her composure, she retrieved her robe, put it on and tied the narrow, ribbonlike belt. The garment was scarcely a shield against his predatory gaze, but the operation gave her a few moments to think. Returning to the fire, she put her back to it, warming herself.

"You're right," she said calmly. "I *was* carried away by the moment. And it does seem as though we share some kind of basic animal attraction."

He frowned. "I'm not an eighteen-year-old kid, Annalise. Give me credit for at least some discrimination. I don't have sex with every woman on the street who piques my interest. You've been part of my life forever. And you're incredibly warm and lovely."

She forced a smile. "At the moment, the jury's out on *warm,* but thank you for the compliment."

"Something happened between us," he said doggedly, his fierce gaze daring her to disagree.

"Yes." *Understatement of the year.* "Here's the thing, Sam. I don't really have the time or the inclination to get involved with anybody right now, much less the grandson of my most recent client. You were only planning to be here overnight, two at the most…right?"

"I'd say my schedule is pretty much down the tubes at the moment. You may be stuck with me for a while."

The weird little happy flutter her heart performed was

too "middle school girl" to take seriously. "That's not a valid reason for doing something stupid."

"Didn't seem stupid to me. It felt pretty damned wonderful."

"There's more to life than feeling good."

"Wow, Annalise. When did you turn into a Puritan?"

He was striking back. Trying to provoke. But the words hurt. She looked at him, really looked at him. The whole package was overwhelming. In Charlottesville she could write him off as just another handsome, successful businessman. Here, alone in a remote house, trapped by a winter storm, he looked like the kind of man who could keep a woman safe, no matter the circumstances.

She didn't need a keeper. As the lone Wolff female, she had grown up strong, resilient, entirely capable of steering her own life. But when it came to understanding the kind of feminine ways that drew a man in for the long haul, Annalise was clueless.

Sam, by his own admission, was looking to settle down, to start a family. Even if he played house with Annalise until the blizzard abated, he'd be going back to Charlottesville soon, trolling for a nice, sweet, amenable kind of gal to cook him meat loaf, defer to his wishes and run his house barefoot and pregnant.

Annalise had grown up in the South. She knew the stereotype. And she knew many wonderful women who could hold down full-time jobs and still be damned good mothers and wives. The problem was, Annalise wasn't one of them.

"I'm not a Puritan," she said. "I love sex."

"Prove it."

"Oh, good Lord. Does that line work for you at your age?"

He grinned. And the sexy flash of white teeth literally made her knees week. When he took two steps in her direction, she was trapped. Flames to the back of her, fire to the front. "Kiss me again, darlin'," he said. "Let me keep you warm."

Impossible. Utterly impossible not to respond this time. He scooped her into his arms and whispered nonsensical endearments as he proceeded to kiss her senseless.

Time. She needed time. How could she formulate a thought when his talented fingers were doing amazing things to her aching breasts? Breathing became problematic. Her lips felt puffy and bruised. All she wanted to do was kiss him more.

He braced one hard, long thigh between her thighs, and the firm pressure there took every last bit of self-control she possessed and tossed it to the winds. She had never been one to second-guess her decisions. Confidence and boldness had taken her far in business and in life.

But holy heck, what was she supposed to do in this situation?

"Sam?" She leaned backward in his tight embrace as far as she could, trying to get his attention.

He took advantage of the position to bend and capture one silk-clad nipple and nip it with his teeth. "Sam!"

The moaning cry finally got through to him. He straightened, his face flushed, his shirt awry thanks to her frantic need to touch his chest. Everything about him was disheveled, earthy, intent on carnal pursuits. Even his eyes were cloudy and unfocused.

"What?" he growled, his sexual frustration palpable.

"We have to agree on something."

He released her, bent at the waist and stared at the floor, clearly in pain. "God give me strength. You are the most ball-busting female I've ever met. Make up your mind, damn it. Do you want me or not?"

She rapped her knuckles on his head. "Don't talk to

me like that. You started this insanity. Yes. I want you. But only for the moment. Only while you're in this house. Got it?"

When he straightened and faced her, a shiver of primal feminine apprehension danced through her veins. Here was a man at the end of his rope. And he looked as if he would as soon strangle her with it than let go.

"Are you seriously negotiating a relationship at this god-damn moment?"

"There is no relationship," she shouted, stung by his incredulity. "All we're going to do is indulge in wild monkey sex. No strings."

"Strings…" He repeated the word, his mouth pursed as he tried to decipher her meaning.

"Tell me you get what I'm saying." She didn't understand exactly why she was pushing so hard. Perhaps because she couldn't bear the thought of another half-dozen years of heartache in the aftermath of an encounter with Sam Ely.

His eyes narrowed, he straightened to his full height and his chest rose and fell with each harsh breath. "Here's what I get," he said softly, the words forced through clenched teeth. "I get that you're crazy. Or maybe this is an act you put on to drive men insane so they'll grovel at your feet. But yes. I get it. Hell, sweetheart, I'll sign over my soul to the devil on the spot if you'll take off that gown."

She licked her lips. "Well, okay then." It was rather heady to have a man so intent on ravishing her. Thank God she wasn't a totally inexperienced virgin. That little detail had been taken care of during a sad and disappointing college encounter that had never been repeated.

She had *wanted* to lose her virginity…so that she could understand what the other girls were talking and giggling about. So that she could be part of their charmed inner circle.

As an eighteen-year-old college freshman, she had thought that becoming a woman in the physical sense would help her understand what it meant to be a girl. But when it was all said and done, she was still Annalise Wolff. Impatient. Driven. And far too confident and assertive for most guys to want a serious relationship.

She dated. A lot. Men liked the external package. And she was not a nun. But no one ever interested her enough to go the distance. Even in bed, she'd felt a sense of failure. Perhaps because the earth never shook and the fireworks never boomed.

Now it had come to this. She waited impatiently for Sam to take her in his arms and undress her. Arousal danced and twisted in her lower abdomen, and her heartbeat skittered out of control. She held out her arms. "Say something, damn it. Or are we going to stand here all night?" She was too agitated to worry about her language at this point.

He shrugged, his expression calculating…like a tiger eyeing a mouse. "Take off the gown."

The blunt words sent moisture blooming between her thighs.

"But I thought you would—"

"Now, Annalise. Slowly. Make me wait. Tease me. Taunt me."

The guttural commands were something new. She didn't know Sam had it in him to be so deliciously barbaric. But she liked it.

Feeling his stare like a hot brand, she shrugged out of the robe and tossed it onto a chair. Now there was no disguising her excitement. Her tightly furled nipples actually hurt. She wanted his hands on her skin, everywhere.

Feeling a bit foolish, but breathless with excitement, she put one hand over her breasts, and with the other hand slid the narrow straps of the gown down first one shoulder and then the other. Releasing each arm completely was a little more awkward than she would have liked, but she gave herself points for bravado.

Sam was transfixed, his entire body tense, hands fisted at his hips. "I want to see your breasts. Lower the top."

For a woman who liked being in charge in almost every situation, it was surprisingly comfortable to cede control. Despite Sam's arrogant demands, she realized that in a deeper sense, she was in the driver's seat.

Feeling faint and giddy, she took the bodice of her gown and dragged it to her waist. Someone gasped. Him? Her? It didn't matter. Sam's gob-smacked response went a long way toward making up for the past. She knew he had seen his fair share of naked women, so his reaction to her no-more-than-average breasts was a balm to her battered ego.

He cocked his head, arms folded across his chest. "You're not done."

The heat from the fire singed her back, warming the silk against her skin. She felt exotic, dangerous. Never in the occasional fantasies she'd allowed herself had Sam looked at her in quite this way.

She put her hands in the sides of the gown and shimmied it down her hips. Stepping out of the pile of ruby cloth and kicking it aside, she removed her exotic slippers and faced him bravely. "I seem to be doing all the work," she said, mesmerized by the enormous bulge beneath his fly.

Sam swallowed, the muscles in his throat rippling, betraying the fact that he was deeply invested in this moment. "Do you want me, Annalise?"

Here it was. A chance for revenge. An opportunity to

take that dreadful memory of his rejection and incinerate it. All she had to do was walk out of the room.

She'd have a better chance of baking cookies and serving tea to the Queen of England. Nothing short of an earthquake could have made her call a halt to this wonderful madness. "Yes," she said. "I believe that I do."

Time began to move in slow motion. Even the sounds of the fire muted to a faint murmur. She held out a hand. "I *would* ask *your room or mine,* but neither sounds appealing at the moment. Do you have any ideas?"

"For you, Princess, always."

With one lingering look at her nudity, he stepped away long enough to rob a nearby cupboard of its stash of throws…a blanket, several afghans and one tattered, faded quilt. As Annalise watched, amused and touched by his urgency, he fashioned a makeshift bed in front of the hearth. Grabbing a pillow from the sofa, he tossed it down on the pile and then added a couple more logs and tinder on top of the coals until the fire blazed hot and orangey-red.

Annalise had scooted out of his way while he worked, but now he dragged her back with a challenging stare that said louder than words what he expected of her. She joined him, limbs trembling, and somewhere found the acting skills to emulate a woman who knew her way around the bedroom. "Put your hands in your back pockets, Sam."

He hesitated, but obeyed. "That's askin' a lot, sweetheart. You're one hell of a temptation."

"We'll get there," she promised. With fumbling fingers, she unfastened the buttons of his shirt. Two years ago she had spent six months in Europe touring every major museum from Paris to Rome. Never had she seen a work of art that rivaled Sam's broad, hard chest.

Hard muscles rippled beneath golden skin. An arrow of dark brown hair bisected his rib cage on the way to his belt buckle. When she had the temerity to taste one cop-per-colored nipple, he cursed.

His hands fisted in her hair, dragging her face up to his for a kiss. "God, you make me burn."

It didn't sound entirely like a compliment.

He ravaged her mouth, left love bites at her throat. She wanted him as naked as she was, but she barely had time to catch her breath, much less make demands. When she tried to open the fly of his jeans, he manacled her wrists with one big hand and held them behind her back.

The overt dominance of the action dragged her more deeply into the spell that swirled around them both. She could have broken the hold. She knew that. And he prob-ably knew it as well. But the force of his hunger demanded her compliance, and her own need fed from his.

"Please, Sam," she begged, arching into him. "I want to touch you."

Finally, reluctantly, he released her long enough to rip off his socks and remove his jeans in a harried, one-footed dance. His sex sprang forth eagerly, its length and girth a thing of beauty. The longer she stared, the more it grew.

"Sam Ely," she breathed, feeling a touch of maidenly vapors. "You're a stud."

He blushed. And the sight of his red throat and ruddy cheekbones hurt something deep inside her chest. He was just so damned cute.

Unfortunately, he didn't give her much time to appre-ciate his masculine attributes. Before she could lodge a protest, he scooped her into his arms and deposited her gently on their makeshift bed. With both living room doors closed, the space had long since warmed up, and even if it hadn't, Annalise was sure she wouldn't have noticed the cold.

He hovered over her on one knee. "I don't know how

long I'll last. You've pushed me pretty close to the edge."
Suddenly, dismay darkened his expression. "Oh, hell. I've
got condoms, but they're upstairs."

She saw him contemplate the long frigid path to protec-
tion. And sympathized. "I'm on the pill," she said hopefully, "and I'm okay as far as…well, you know what I
mean." The brazen-woman act fell apart when it came to
discussing such topics.

His face lightened. "I had a physical last month. A-okay.
You can trust me, Annalise. I hope you know that."

"I do," she whispered. Without waiting for an invitation,
she reached out and took him in her hand, measuring the
firm, swollen flesh with inner wonder. If sculptors created
guys like Sam, the museums would be a lot more crowded.

His eyes closed at the first brush of her fingers. He felt
amazingly hard and disarmingly smooth and silky. But
would all that *maleness* fit? Her thighs clenched in something that was a cross between breathless excitement and
genuine apprehension.

Stroking him tentatively, she caught her breath when
he went rigid and found release in her hand, warm liquid
leaking through her fingers and dribbling onto her belly.

He groaned. "Annalise, I'm sorry. Let's try that again."
Very matter-of-factly he used a corner of one thin blanket to clean her and himself. She was abashed, unused to
such easy intimacy. But his tenderness charmed and disarmed her.

His shaft was still mostly erect, definitely firm enough
to get the job done. But instead of moving over and into
her, he knelt between her legs and grinned the kind of
grin that guaranteed a girl in trouble. "You're not saying
anything."

Suddenly, she wanted to cover her breasts with her
hands, but knew that would elicit a hoot of derision from

her beautifully naked lover. "You seem to have everything under control," she said. "Knock yourself out."

The grin broadened, and he stretched out on his side, tucking his torso between her thighs so he could reach what he was after.

Annalise closed her eyes and groaned inwardly. What he was about to do was both terrifying and wickedly wonderful. She'd spent her entire life protecting her deepest emotions. Only once had she dared to wear her heart on her sleeve, and it had been shattered by this very man.

Now she was allowing him the utmost intimacy, and she wasn't at all sure she could separate sexual bliss from a deeper, far more fragile emotion. It was one thing to let him see she desired him. But far more dangerous to expose the reality that she had never stopped loving him.

The first pass of his lips brought her hips off the floor. Her fists gripped the soft covers beneath her to find an anchor. She'd been fastidious and guarded in her few physical relationships up until this moment. Never had she permitted a man to get this close. Never had she imagined how good this would feel. She wasn't naive. She read books. Saw movies. Oral sex was a natural part of lovemaking, even if she'd always drawn a line to hold men at bay.

The oddly clinical commentary in her brain shut down when Sam used his thumbs to part the folds of her sex so his talented tongue could concentrate on the spot that begged for his attention. He tasted her delicately, fine-tuning his technique in reaction to her wiggling hips.

He licked the inside of her thigh, bit gently, laid his head on her belly. The weight of him anchored her in a spinning world. Without volition, one of her hands unclenched and found its way to Sam's hair, sliding into the thick, wavy layers.

She traced the curves of his skull, drunk with the pleasure of being able to touch him at will.

Now he used his fingers, plucking delicately, stroking as if he had all the time in the world. Her belly tightened. An ache coalesced deep inside her. "Stop," she breathed, the word barely audible. "Not like this. I want you inside me when I come."

Lifting his head, he looked at her, eyes solemn, an errant lock of hair falling over his forehead. He looked young and carefree and as tempting as the devil. "Whatever you want, Annalise."

He went to his knees and leaned forward, one hand on either side of her. The heat from his body felt like a warm blanket. Nudging her knees a little wider, he fit the head of his erection to her damp core and pushed.

Her heels dug into the blanket. Eyelids fluttered shut. Neck arched. Breathing halted. The sensation of fullness was both novel and overwhelming. "Sam. Oh, Sam." How many times had she dreamed of this moment? And been foolish enough to let the fantasies keep her from forming relationships with other men.

She hadn't consciously saved herself for Sam. After all, most of the time she was able to convince herself that she despised him.

But not now. Not like this. Her throat burned and her eyes stung. Perfection. Desire met and sated. Damp skin to damp skin. Heart to heart. So badly did she want him to say he loved her that it was a sharp pain squeezing her chest.

His eyes were closed, his face a mask of intensity, of carnal pleasure. The pace increased. His hips pistoned, driving him deeper into her welcoming body.

Her fingernails scored his shoulders. Her legs wrapped

around his waist. He reached beneath her and canted her hips for one last desperate push.

Something exploded inside her, ecstasy and shock and a physical release so deep and utterly breathtaking that she lost a few seconds of reality in the maelstrom.

She heard Sam shout. Seconds later, he slumped on top of her, stealing what little oxygen was left in her lungs. Her arms clung to him automatically. She was beyond rational conversation. Nothing seemed real. Not the place. Not the feelings. Not even the big, raw-boned man smothering her with his hot skin, ragged breath and beautiful body.

As delight winnowed away with the ticking of the clock on the mantel, panic set in. What had she done? It had taken her years to recover from her first romantic debacle with Sam Ely. At twenty-one she had been mature for her age in terms of goal-setting and a life plan. And though some might say in retrospect that she'd had nothing more than a youthful crush on a man much older than she was, Annalise knew the truth.

She had been in love. The real deal. Despite what had happened back then…and even through the intervening years of guarded hostility on her part, based on tonight's utterly unexpected, and unbelievably wonderful events, the truth was impossible to evade.

Annalise Wolff was still in love with Sam Ely.

Six

The power came back on just as faint evidence of dawn chased away dark shadows and painted the room with gray. Annalise yawned, her brain fuzzy. The night before, Sam had gone through the house and turned off all the light switches before they retired, so the only evidence that twenty-first century conveniences had returned was the gentle, reassuring hum of the heat system cranking up.

She allowed herself one last moment to savor the odd but lovely sensation of sleeping with a man. Sam radiated heat. She was curled into his side with one bent leg across his hips and her face tucked against his chest. Sometime during the wee hours he had pulled the covers on top of them.

She didn't know what to do, and that was such an anomaly, she felt mildly claustrophobic. Ordinarily, she *always* knew what to do. Sometimes she mapped out a plan. More often than not, she plunged ahead, full speed, confident that she could handle whatever might be coming down the track.

But that was in business. Her work was her life, a sad thing for a woman her age to admit, but there it was. She loved the challenge of space design, of color, of texture. And she loved helping people create their own nests. Especially since many of her clients had no idea what they really wanted when they signed on.

Recently, she had spent more and more time at Wolff Mountain. It was gratifying to see her family, one at a time, finding happiness after the childhood of tragedy they had shared as a common cup. Even her big brother, Devlyn, had lately managed to lay some of his demons to rest when he reconnected with quiet, patient Gillian.

For Annalise, it wasn't that easy. Her brothers and cousins loved her. She knew that. And her father and uncle did, as well. But despite the close relationships they all shared, Annalise was the only female. How did she say to one of her big, masculine brothers that she was frightened by the specter of never finding her soul mate? How did she ask for advice on becoming a softer, more feminine woman?

Happily, she had a quartet of new in-laws…or at least Gillian would be one soon. But although each of her new-found sisters was extremely gracious and loving, Annalise didn't know them well enough to open a vein and let them see her insecurities.

Sam murmured in his sleep, drawing her attention back to his classic profile and warm-man smell. She would bottle that aroma if she could. His lashes lay dark on his cheeks, and his chest rose and fell with deep, regular breathing.

Slowly, stealthily, she extracted herself from muscular arms and scrambled to her feet. It was no wonder he was dead to the world. He'd been up for hours, either trying to get warm, or later, turning Annalise's world upside down with a sexual marathon that had included one last coupling as the fire died. The memory drew a quiet groan of amazement from her throat. At least she had gotten a couple of hours of sleep *before* creeping through the house to confront a possible intruder.

There had been an intruder, all right. And one equally as dangerous as a rogue bear. The problem with Sam was that he seemed on the surface to be the perfect guy.

As long as she overlooked the fact that he was ready to play daddy. The thought of having Sam's baby both mesmerized and terrified her. That was why she had given him an ultimatum regarding sex. She had too much self-preservation to buy into the fiction that she and Sam could ever work as a couple.

It took every ounce of willpower she possessed to don her gown and robe instead of waking Sam deliberately and watching his eyes heat with passion. One of her slippers had slid under a chair, but she finally located it. The sensible plan was to take a shower, and then pick a room in which to get started sketching out some ideas.

The fee Sam's grandparents were offering her was extremely generous. But Annalise had enough ego to be tempted even more by the prospect of the magazine spread. She'd learned the tenets of ambition and hard work at her daddy's knee, and one day, if she chose to, she had the option of joining Devlyn in running the family business.

She doubted she would ever want to…at least not directly, but it was nice to know that no one in the family would think it odd. She had never faced any kind of discrimination in the Wolff "pack" for being a girl. Well, except for the fact that her father showered her with gifts and encouraged her to order a new wardrobe each season.

She was pretty sure he felt guilty for cloistering her for all those years. An all-access pass to high fashion was his way of making amends. It was a nice perk. But going to school as a child and making friends would have been even nicer.

Sam never moved as she tiptoed to the door and opened it stealthily. With one last wistful glance at the man in front of the fire, she slipped out across the hall and into the safety of her bedroom.

Sam waited until he heard the door close to sigh deeply and roll onto his back. He had awakened when Annalise was dressing. Rubbing eyes that were gritty from lack of sleep, he forced himself to face the fact that she had run out on him. So much for warm cuddling and perhaps further bonding over morning sex.

Given her behavior in the last sixty seconds, Annalise was not interested. As rejections went, her dismissal was quiet…polite even. Sam weighed the lump of lead in his gut and found it to be a mix of disappointment and hurt. Confidence had never been a problem for him. But if he were dead honest, he would have to acknowledge the fact that he felt embarrassed and at a loss as to how to approach the coming day.

He got to his feet, nude, and was not surprised to find he was still hard. It was inevitable. Annalise, despite her mercurial temperament and frequent antipathy, did it for him. Everything about her appealed to his basic male instincts. Her beauty drew him in, but the challenge of wrangling with her kept him interested.

He'd never been one to use a pretty girl on his arm to shore up his masculinity. He was a guy. Looks mattered. To some extent. But a shallow, self-centered female bored him. And boredom was a buzzkill as far as he was concerned.

It seemed pointless to dress when he was headed upstairs to clean up. But then again, he didn't want to run in to his houseguest while in the buff. Time to regroup and make a plan.

After a long, blessedly hot shower, he dressed rapidly and peeked out the window. Snow as far as the eye could see. Sam had mixed feelings about being stranded. On the one hand, it was an iron-clad excuse to spend more time with Annalise. But conversely, if she proved to be even more prickly than usual in the aftermath of their lovemaking, their living situation was quickly going to become too close for comfort.

When he made his way downstairs, he found evidence of Annalise's presence in the form of an empty mug and cereal bowl tucked away in the dishwasher. He fell on the fresh pot of coffee with a mental hallelujah. Thank God she knew enough not to ruin this. After two cups, he felt marginally more alert.

He had plenty of work to do. And he needed to check in at the office. But all he could think about was finding Annalise.

It wasn't hard to locate her. She had moved her iPod dock to the back of the house where she was working, but this time, the music was dialed down to a far lower volume. He followed the sound to what was known as the library, though in reality, his grandfather used it to house his vintage pool table.

When Sam opened the door that was partially ajar, he found Annalise perched on a ladder photographing small sections of an intricate crown molding.

He frowned, noting the rickety wooden rungs that should have necessitated tossing the thing years ago. "What in the hell are you doing?"

She froze, and then slowly turned her head, casting him a cool, inscrutable look. Full-on ice princess. Damn.

"This is original as far as I can tell. I'm texting a friend of mine who specializes in this kind of thing. He'll let me know what he thinks." She laid the phone she'd been using to take pictures on the top of the ladder. "Did you need something?"

You. The word hovered on his lips. He swallowed it back. "Not really. When will you break for lunch? I thought I'd throw together a pot of chili and some cornbread."

Was it his imagination, or did she pale slightly. "You can do that?"

"Cook, you mean? Well, yeah. I've been a bachelor for a long time."

She gnawed her lower lip. "Noon, then…or later. Your call."

He watched, frustrated, as she returned her attention to the task at hand, effectively dismissing him. She was wearing what for Annalise Wolff were probably casual clothes. Khakis, silver leather ballet flats, a crisp white cotton blouse and a thin black cashmere cardigan tied around her shoulders. Her hair was secured at the nape of her neck, leaving a long, thick ponytail to cascade down her back.

For a split second, he remembered what that hair looked like spread across his chest, his legs, his… He gulped inwardly. "I could teach you," he blurted out.

This time, she half turned her entire body, threatening the stability of her perch. Wariness dueled with interest in her expressive eyes. "Teach me to…"

"Make chili." He felt his neck heat. "If you want to learn. It's not hard." The genesis for his impulsive invitation wasn't clear. But something about the surprised pleasure in her smile made him glad he had asked.

"I'd love to," she said simply. "As long as I can't muck it up too badly."

"Like how?"

She shrugged. "You know. Food poisoning. Too much salt."

He grinned, feeling a return of the euphoria he had experienced in the middle of the night. "Meet me in the kitchen in half an hour. Trust me, Princess. You'll be in good hands."

Annalise worked steadily, one part of her brain dedicated to the disciplines of measuring, calculating, planning. The other hemisphere, the one that acknowledged and ruefully accepted her ill-advised infatuation with Sam Ely, seemed intent on translating each of his statements into a sexual innuendo.

You'll be in good hands. Did he intend the erotic subtext? Probably not. She was hyperaware of the fact that she and Sam Ely had recently become lovers. But such nocturnal calisthenics were no doubt par for the course with Sam. To him, Annalise was nothing more or less than a willing and available woman. Available. Could she be any more of a cliché?

Feeling disgruntled and exhausted and excited in equal measures, she found her way to the kitchen at the appointed time. Sam, standing at the stove, turned to face her. "Ah, there you are. I was just getting started. Come here and supervise the meat."

She hovered in the doorway, all thoughts of food forgotten. Sam was too damned sexy for his own good. He was dressed much as he had been the day before, only with a different shirt. This time, hunter green flannel stretched across the broad contours of his chest and shoulders. It was still hard to get used to his new look.

For years she had known Sam Ely as the sleek, handsome, *über*masculine architect with the expensive Italian tailored suits and the knack for sartorial perfection.

He reeked of money and success from his pricey leather shoes to the high-tech Rolex on his broad masculine wrist.

But this man, well, hell…she didn't know what to make of him at all. He was warm and approachable and nurturing. And about as dangerous as a grizzly bear basking in the sun.

One wrong move, and she'd be toast.

Shoring up her defenses, she crossed to where he stood. "Show me what to do."

Sam stepped back and handed her the wooden spoon he'd been using. "Stir it occasionally and break up the bigger clumps of meat. When all the pink is gone, it will be ready." As she took her position, he flanked her, his arms coming around from behind, his right hand settling over hers as she pushed the meat blindly.

"Like this," he said. The scent of his shower soap muddled her thoughts. She wanted to toss the spoon aside and kiss him senseless. The warmth of him at her back made her hands shake. Gripping the utensil tightly, she tried to pretend it was nothing out of the ordinary to play chef with the man who had seduced her in front of a fire only hours before.

His fingers gripped hers and released, his voice hoarse as he spoke near her ear. "You've got the hang of it."

To her intense disappointment, he stepped away, moving to open cans of tomato soup and sauce. She watched him out of the corner of her eye. The fact that he wasn't producing some exotic sauce from scratch made her feel marginally better.

Suddenly, she realized that the pan was sizzling far more than it had been a few moments before. "Um, Sam?" At about the same moment she said his name, the hot grease popped and crackled. A splatter hit her forearm, and she yelped, dropping the spoon and sending bits of browned ground beef flying everywhere.

Sam grabbed her wrist and pulled it beneath a cooling stream of water from the faucet. Already the sting was subsiding. Leaving her for a moment, he turned the stove off and moved the skillet to another burner.

"Are you all right?" He took her hand and lifted her arm for his inspection.

"It's okay. Just a red spot. Sorry I overreacted." She tugged until he released her.

Sam shook his head. "It had to hurt. My fault for not turning down the heat."

"I told you I'm hopeless in the kitchen." She was mortified to feel the sting of tears.

He cocked his head, studying her face, his whiskey-colored eyes seeing far more than they should. "It's no big deal, Annalise. You've got enough money to *hire* people to cook for you."

"That's not the point."

"Then what *is* the point?"

"Women are supposed to be able to cook."

He opened his mouth, closed it and sighed. "I'm trying not to trivialize your concern," he said, "but that's a ridiculous, outdated stereotype."

"No," she said, sticking out her chin. "It's not. We *say* men and women are equal now that it's the twenty-first century, but when push comes to shove, my sex is supposed to be gentle and kind and proficient in the domestic arts."

"Oh, good Lord, Annalise. Do you hear yourself? So you can't cook. Who the hell cares? If it's that important to you, take lessons. But if you see this as some deficiency in you as a woman, you're nuts."

She stared at him. "I'll bet you a thousand dollars that your mother and grandmother are amazing cooks."

He shook his head in disgust, bending to wipe up the meat she had flung willy-nilly across the floor. "I refuse to get into this."

She nudged his butt with the toe of her shoe. "Because you know I'm right. You've grown up with two generations of women who can plant gardens and make casseroles and bake birthday cakes without a mix."

He straightened, tossing the wad of paper towels in the garbage. "And you didn't. Is that it?"

When he went on the attack, she lost focus. "Not exactly," she muttered. "Forget it. I'm going back to work. Call me when lunch is ready."

"Not so fast." He pulled her into his arms so rapidly, she actually felt dizzy for a moment. Plastered against his chest, she felt every one of his ribs, heard each heartbeat, registered the ragged tenor of his breathing.

When she opened her mouth to protest, he covered it with his.

He went in deep, without apology, staking a claim. Making clear what he wanted. Sam Ely was hungry, but she had a feeling that chili was far down on his list.

"What are you doing?" she gasped, struggling for air between frantic kisses.

He tangled his fist in her ponytail and used the tension to tip back her head so he could nibble her neck. "If you have to ask, I must be doing it wrong."

Before she could assimilate a thought or form a protest, he had scooped her into his arms and was striding out of the kitchen and across the hall to her bedroom. The door was ajar a couple of inches. He kicked it open, endangering ancient hinges.

"Sam!" The single syllable ended on a whimpering sigh as he set her on her feet and cupped her breasts with both hands.

"Don't talk," he begged. "Just let me do this."

This was full-out, desperation-fueled seduction.

And at the moment, Annalise couldn't think of a single reason to quibble about the method. Sam undressed her reverently, but with enough clumsiness to betray his need for haste. His hands found every soft curve, every bit of damp skin, every responsive group of nerves. By the time she was bare-ass naked and flat on her back, Sam was stripping off his clothes.

When he came down beside her, the antique bed squeaked in protest. Manufactured long before the advent of queen-size mattresses, the fit was cozy. He stroked between her legs, finding her damp and ready. "You make me crazy, Annalise."

"The feeling is mutual," she muttered. Tired of waiting, she reached for him and closed her fingers around hard silky flesh. Sam's quick catch of breath elated her. She squeezed gently, tracing the vein on the underside of his shaft with her thumb. Despite what had happened between the two of them in the wee hours, she still felt clumsy and unsure of herself. Lacking domestic skills was one thing, but the specter of possibly being bad in bed took insecurity to a whole new level.

To most people who knew her, Annalise Wolff was a sharp-edged, assertive, take-no-prisoners businesswoman. She'd been told to her face that she intimidated competitors, particularly if they were female. It wasn't something she aspired to or even practiced.

Her family had taught her to be confident and capable in business. Wolff men were all that and more. And they had reared Annalise both by precept and example to be one of the pack.

Though she had mastered the art of "looking" like a sexy female, no one had tutored her in the finer points of how to transform the essence of who she was from a tom-boy child into an admirable woman. Except for the female staff, she had been completely isolated by her sex and from her sex. Things most girls learned by osmosis had never registered on Annalise's radar. She had held herself up to a masculine standard and never realized she was short-changing an entire part of who she was.

Beneath her touch, Sam's rigid flesh twitched and grew. Apparently, she was doing something right. He touched her thigh. "Lift your leg over mine," he said, his voice rough with sexual intent. She did as he asked, feeling a momentary frisson of unease at the position. So open. So unprotected. Sam angled his hips and entered her slowly, grabbing her hip to thrust deeper.

The penetration was shallower than last night, but con-versely, far more risky. Now she and Sam lay face-to-face, their breaths mingling…her ragged sighs, his groans. His gaze locked with hers. "I like seeing you like this," he said.

"Like what?" This was why people closed their eyes during sex. Too much communication was scary.

"Relaxed. Compliant."

"Trust me," she squeaked as he delved farther and hit a sensitive spot, "I'm not relaxed." The tightly wound spiral in the base of her abdomen clamored for attention. Sam's left arm lay curled beneath her neck. With his free hand, he plucked lazily at her nipple, adding fuel to the inferno that throbbed between her legs.

His lazy grin made her want to slap him, or kiss him, or both. "You will be," he promised.

She squeezed him with inner muscles that took over the reins in naughty intent. "Show me," she whispered, the words in challenge.

Every trace of humor fled his face to be replaced by sheer male determination. With one arm, he dragged her closer for a kiss that was carnal and curious and calamitous. With the other, he drew her even more tightly into the cradle of his thighs, melding their bodies in a frantic hold. His tongue tangled with hers, his chest heaving, skin damp with perspiration. "Come for me, Princess. Let go…now."

That he could coax a climax from her at will was both exhilarating and terrifying. She slammed into the peak and crashed over it with the force of a speeding train, her senses all focused on that one perfect moment.

Sam held her in a bruising grip as he shouted and shuddered at almost the same instant.

"Sweetheart," he gasped. "You're gonna kill me before the weekend is out."

Annalise wrote off his dramatic words to postcoital hyperbole. After all, her hands-on experience with the erotic arts wouldn't fill a paragraph on a résumé. He was exaggerating in order to ensure that she would agree to another round later.

But even as she lectured herself inwardly, she couldn't help but feel a smug sense of feminine power that she had satisfied him. Moments later, she winced when he withdrew, not that it hurt, but because he broke the wonderful feeling of togetherness that was like nothing she had ever experienced.

Sam made up for the loss by urging her onto her side and spooning her back, one of his arms cradling her head and the other tucked beneath her breasts. She allowed herself one dreamy smile, since he couldn't see her face. If she could maintain the fiction of sex as recreation, she could protect her heart.

He sighed, the warm puff of air brushing the nape of her neck like a caress. In the silence, she couldn't tell if he had drifted off to sleep or was lost in thought. His words, when they finally came, were totally unexpected, though they were slurred with drowsiness. "Tell me, Annalise, after all these years, what do you remember about your mother?"

Seven

Sam would have to be completely insensitive, or at least a fool, not to note the moment when her body went rigid. And he was neither. Cursing his stupidity, he waited, wishing like hell he could retract the question. He'd spent the better part of an hour coaxing the prickly princess into a warm, malleable mood, and then he'd destroyed it all with his damned curiosity.

Bit by bit, she relaxed. But not like before. Not at all. "Very little," she said in a voice that was suspiciously casual. "I was really young when she died. Most of the memories are from photographs or from things my brothers told me. My father has never really talked about her."

"You missed out on a lot," he said, his heart aching for a bereft little girl who would have been far too young to understand what death meant. The finality. The utter cruelty.

He felt her shrug. "I did fine," she insisted. Did she

realize that her right hand held the sheet in a white-knuckled grip?

He should have dropped the subject. He knew it was the right thing to do. But he was desperate to understand what made Annalise Wolff tick, and his window of opportunity was very narrow. Particularly if the temperatures outside began rising, as predicted.

"I know what it is to be without a parent," he said quietly. "It's not the same as death. I understand the difference, I do. But when my mother took me away from my father, all the way to south Alabama, I felt as if he had died. Phone calls were difficult because of his work schedule and my bedtime. I wanted him to tuck me into bed at night. To read me a story. Divorce was just a word. It meant nothing to me. I was angry for a long time. Screwed up at school on purpose. Gave my mom hell. But in the end, I had to adapt."

She turned her head and kissed the sensitive flesh of his upper arm. "I'm sorry."

"I know they had issues I couldn't understand. I still don't for that matter. Neither of them has ever remarried."

"So why did they separate?"

"Hell if I know. But that's why I'm determined never to do that to my kids. I want a real family. If my parents had stayed together, I might have been lucky enough to have siblings like you do."

Annalise sighed. "My brothers and cousins are everything to me. I can't imagine not having them in my life. We fuss and fight sometimes, even as adults, but they have my back. It must suck being an only child."

"Yeah, well, this conversation wasn't supposed to be all about me. I'm trying to let you know that I experienced a tiny bit of what you went through. And I'm sorry, too. A little girl needs her mother."

"It was no great loss," she said, her voice without inflection. "My mother wasn't a very nice person."

The flat, one-dimensional syllables made his scalp tingle and gooseflesh erupt on his arms. Such deliberate lack of emotion surely hid unimaginable hurt.

Annalise sat up, her narrow, pale-skinned back all he could see of her. She gathered the quilt to protect her nudity and stood gracefully. "I need to get back to work. Please let me know when lunch is ready."

And then she locked herself in the bathroom.

Damn, damn and damn. Pushing her emotionally was the dumbest idea he'd had in a while. Sam had visited Wolff Castle enough times over the years to realize that the family tragedy was kept under lock and key. Neither the older generation nor their offspring wore their hearts on their sleeves.

No one discussed the tragic kidnappings, the senseless shootings, or the move, en masse, to their mountain asylum. It was as if by denying the past, they could pretend it never happened.

Case in point, Annalise. She had perfected the art of avoidance. As far as she was concerned, that kiss she gave him years ago never happened, either. Which pissed off Sam. He wasn't going to let her forget it. At one time, she had wanted him. And her body still did, even though her mind and heart were doing their damnedest to remain uninvolved.

To put it bluntly, Annalise was having sex with him like some men would. Strictly physically. With no intention of entering into any kind of long-term relationship. Hell, Sam himself had approached sex that way when he was younger.

But that was then and this was now. Slowly, the light was beginning to dawn. He might want more from Annalise Wolff than he had realized at first glance. He might want it all.

That notion spooked him so badly he bolted from her bedroom, clothes in hand. Was he insane? As he redressed and did his best to salvage the chili, his heart pounded in his chest. He didn't have the luxury of "trying" a relationship with Annalise. If it crashed and burned, he would have to face the music from the older generation. His dad, her father, Uncle Victor. Not to mention five angry brothers and cousins, any one of whom could go head-to-head with him in a fist fight.

As he sliced bread and buttered it, his brain whirled. It was time to back off. The Weather Channel app on his phone said they should see widespread snowmelt by the day after tomorrow. Sam could be back in Charlottesville in time for dinner that night.

Sex with Annalise had been incredible. Possibly the best of his life. But physical intimacy with her came with a lot of baggage. And he wasn't sure it was worth it.

Lunch was awkward and long. Annalise picked at her chili, though she professed it to be delicious. Her careful politeness emulated the demeanor of a reserved young lady. It was weird. And scary.

Sam wolfed down his first bowl and went back for seconds, not so much because he was hungry, but for something to do. When they were done, Annalise offered to help clean up. He declined. When she stared at him briefly, her eyes turbulent with unspoken emotion, he almost cracked.

Instead, he turned toward the sink and held his breath until he heard her leave.

Two hours later, he was ready to climb the walls. He had three young, ambitious paid interns back at the office, any one of whom could run the whole operation given half a chance. That they were all at work on a Saturday morning pointed to their determination to succeed. After a spirited conference call to handle a few pressing matters, he bade them goodbye and hung up. He was itchy, and irritable, and, well…hard.

When he gave in and went in search of his guest, he found Annalise in the same room as earlier, back up on the ladder, picking at a corner of wallpaper with a pocket-knife. This time she didn't give him the courtesy of looking up to note his entrance into the room.

Her gaze was focused on the task at hand, as if by peeling back enough layers she might uncover the secrets of the Rosetta Stone. Sam didn't like being ignored.

"What are you doing now?" he asked, his tone a masterpiece of mild interest.

Still no turn of the head. "Trying to determine how many layers of paper are under here. It's possible that the deepest ones might give us something to go on in terms of color."

"You know that my grandmother doesn't have to have everything exactly like it was…even if you could figure that out. She just wants the decor to be in keeping with the time period of the original house. After all, she's not making Pops get rid of this pool table." He reached in the side pocket and pulled out a striped ball, rolling it in his hand. "I learned to play when I was ten years old. And the old man didn't cut me any slack. It took me four summers to finally win a game."

Finally, Annalise gave him her attention, and a tiny, reluctant smile lifted the edges of her lush lips. "I learned at eight," she said. "And I could beat both Devlyn and Gareth by the time I was nine."

His eyebrows went up. "The devil, you say…."

"I'm always up for a wager."

He felt a kick in his chest and his gut simultaneously. When she forgot to be guarded with him, the luminosity of her smile literally took his breath away. He cleared his throat. "Don't you have work to do?"

She came down two rungs. "Are you chicken?"

His eyes narrowed. He knew when he as being hustled. But he had a competitive streak a mile wide, and he wasn't going to let Annalise get the best of him. "I assume you're going to put your money where your mouth is?"

She cocked her head. "I hate to take your cash."

"A thousand dollars."

That made her blink. But in an instant she was back on track, projecting disdain in her deliberately bored expression. "Ten thousand dollars. To be donated to the new school."

"And if I win? When I win," he amended hastily.

"What do you want?"

Suddenly, every cell in his body hummed with sexual energy. *You.* It was a shocking truth. And one he decided not to give voice to. He rocked back on his heels, hands braced in the door frame. "I want to take you to dinner. Somewhere nice. Linen tablecloths. Roses in crystal vases. Soft lighting."

Suspicion etched her delicate features. "I told you I don't like romantic stuff."

"No romance," he said quietly, trying to gauge her mood. "Just a civilized meal between friends."

"Not in Charlottesville."

"Why?"

"You know why. I don't want anyone to see us together and get the wrong idea."

"Then where?"

"D.C.?"

"We'd have to spend the night."

Her cheeks flushed. "Okay, so Roanoke, maybe."

"We're both grown-ups, Annalise. If we want to have a secretive tryst, it's our business."

She nibbled her lower lip, her gaze moody. "Again with the romance. I said no."

"Every woman likes romance. But the point is, it's up to her partner to decide what that means. If I decide to romance you, darlin', you'll never see it coming. Subtlety is my middle name."

She snorted. "You're about as subtle as a Mack truck. In that case, wager accepted. But dinner only. No funny business."

He held up his hands. "You wound me. I'd never try to seduce you without your permission."

"My permission? That will be a cold day in Hades."

His body tightened. Annalise had the heart of a tease. And she played the game well. The problem was, he was pretty sure it was all instinctive. He doubted she knew what her sass and smart mouth did to him.

Without waiting for an invitation, she started pulling balls out of pockets and setting them on the table, the movements of her hands both graceful and efficient.

"Who gets to break?" he asked.

"We'll flip a coin."

Before he could comment, she pulled a dime out of her pocket, shot it in the air and caught it on her forearm, covering it with her free hand. "You call it."

"Heads."

She showed him the result. Tails. Of course. He sighed audibly.

Annalise smirked. "Too bad."

He slouched against the wall as she gathered the balls, racked them and carefully removed the plastic triangle.

⊕HARLEQUIN® READER SERVICE—Here's How It Works:

Accepting your 2 free books and 2 free gifts (gifts valued at approximately $10.00) places you under no obligation to buy anything. You may keep the books and gifts and return the shipping statement marked "cancel". If you do not cancel, about a month later we'll send you 6 additional books and bill you just $4.30 each in the U.S. or $4.99 each in Canada. That's a savings of at least 14% off the cover price. It's quite a bargain! Shipping and handling is just 50¢ per book in the U.S. and 75¢ per book in Canada.* You may cancel at any time, but if you choose to continue, every month we'll send you 6 more books, which you may either purchase at the discount price or return to us and cancel your subscription.

*Terms and prices subject to change without notice. Prices do not include applicable taxes. Sales tax applicable in N.Y. Canadian residents will be charged applicable taxes. Offer not valid in Quebec. All orders subject to credit approval. Credit or debit balances in a customer's account(s) may be offset by any other outstanding balance owed by or to the customer. Please allow 4 to 6 weeks for delivery. Offer available while quantities last.

NO POSTAGE
NECESSARY
IF MAILED
IN THE
UNITED STATES

BUSINESS REPLY MAIL
FIRST-CLASS MAIL   PERMIT NO. 717   BUFFALO, NY

POSTAGE WILL BE PAID BY ADDRESSEE

HARLEQUIN READER SERVICE
PO BOX 1867
BUFFALO NY 14240-9952

If offer card is missing write to: Harlequin Reader Service, P.O. Box 1867, Buffalo NY 14240-1867 or visit www.ReaderService.com

HD-L7-10-1/13

GET FREE BOOKS and FREE GIFTS
WHEN YOU PLAY THE...

Lucky 7

Just scratch off the silver box with a coin. Then check below to see the gifts you get!

SLOT MACHINE GAME!

YES!
I have scratched off the silver box. Please send me the 2 free Harlequin® Desire® books and 2 free gifts for which I qualify. I understand I am under no obligation to purchase any books, as explained on the back of this card.

225/326 HDL FV9H

FIRST NAME | LAST NAME

ADDRESS

APT.# | CITY

STATE/PROV. | ZIP/POSTAL CODE

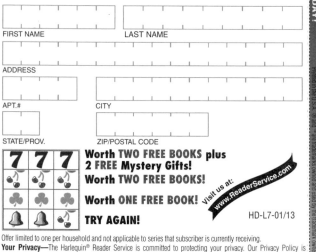

7 7 7   **Worth TWO FREE BOOKS plus 2 FREE Mystery Gifts!**

🍒🍒🍒   **Worth TWO FREE BOOKS!**

♣♣♣   **Worth ONE FREE BOOK!**

🔔🔔🍒   **TRY AGAIN!**

Visit us at: www.ReaderService.com

HD-L7-01/13

DETACH AND MAIL CARD TODAY!

Printed in the U.S.A. ® and ™ are trademarks owned and used by the trademark owner and/or its licensee.

© 2012 HARLEQUIN ENTERPRISES LIMITED

HD-L7-01/13

When she leaned over the table, he recognized his basic handicap. Watching Annalise Wolff shoot pool was guaranteed to turn his brain to mush and make other parts of him, well…not mush.

She moved with a confidence that was beautiful to watch. Sam had played pool with other women. Most of them either refused to break or did so with such a weak shot that the balls remained clumped together. It should have come as no surprise to him that Annalise was not like other women.

Ignoring him completely, she chalked her cue, lined up her shot and sent the cue ball slamming into the tightly packed stripes and solids. A trio of the latter slid into three pockets with a precision that made his jaw drop.

She paused to give him one sly, taunting smile over her shoulder before returning to her game and running the table. When nothing remained on the felt but a single white ball, she wiggled her shoulders, stretched her hands over her head and lifted an eyebrow. "Your turn, Mr. Ely."

Muttering beneath his breath, he picked out his own cue and told himself to ignore the fact that a beautiful woman stood watching him. Her gaze tracked his every move. Even so, he managed a creditable break, sinking two shots to her three. He lined up the next few, one after another…and made them.

But when he went for the last one, he made the mistake of looking at his adversary. Her unusual blue eyes sparkled with amusement as if lit from within. His pride suffered a nick. So much so that he bobbled the shot and had to suffer the indignity of having Annalise step up and clean the rest of the table.

When it was over, silence reigned.

She replaced her cue in the rack on the wall and flipped

her ponytail back over her shoulder. "Not bad for an old man," she said. "I guess your reflexes are slowing down."

"Didn't anyone ever teach you that you're supposed to let the guy win?"

It was a smart-aleck comment, a tease, a jab. Certainly not a serious rejoinder. But Annalise blanched. And for the briefest of seconds, he saw real distress in her deep, translucent eyes. "Hey," he said quickly, seeking to temper his blunder. "You know I'm kidding, right? You're amazing. If you weren't already swimming in money, you could play this game professionally. It's true that I don't like losing. But I'll have another shot. You beat me fair and square."

She had turned away during his impulsive backpedaling and was now fiddling with a portfolio of notes she'd been working on earlier. He touched her arm, making her face him. When she wouldn't look at him, he took her chin in his hands. Though several moments ticked by, finally her eyes met his.

He stroked her cheeks with his thumbs. "I... Was... Kidding. Get it? No man worth his salt wants a woman to *let* him win at anything."

"You'd be surprised," she whispered. The single tear that clung to her lower lashes refused to fall.

Feeling like the biggest jerk on the planet, he kissed her forehead. "You can't tell me all those wild Wolffs of yours wanted a fake victory."

She chuckled weakly. "Them? No. Daddy and Uncle Vic used to give me five dollars every time I beat one of the boys. My brothers and cousins hated it, but it made them work harder to improve their game. Unfortunately, when I finally went off to college, no one told me the rules had changed."

"What do you mean?"

"My first week on campus I was invited to a frat party

with five or six other girls. The house had a pool table. One of the pledges offered to teach me the game…I guess to show off to his buddies."

"And you beat him."

"Three games in a row. I was too arrogant for my own good." She paused, as if seeing a painful vision known only to her. "He called me a dyke," she said abruptly. "Everyone laughed."

"Jesus, Annalise." He took her in his arms, despite the fact that she was stiff as a board in his embrace. "College guys are unmitigated jerks for the most part. They check their brains when they walk through those ivy-clad arches and don't reclaim them until four years later. He was thinking with something other than his brain, and you showed him up. It wasn't your fault. Good Lord, you should be proud of your talent."

She sniffed, finally relaxing enough to lay her head on his shoulder. "Mine is more luck than skill. I've always had a knack for geometry. I see the angles. It's no big deal."

He shook her gently. "Be proud of who you are. You're an original. A Wolff daughter. One of a kind."

"Sometimes it's lonely," she said quietly.

He froze, stunned to realize that for perhaps the first time, Annalise was trusting him enough to open that closely guarded heart of hers and let him see a glimpse of the marshmallow center inside the crusty shell. "What about your sisters-in-law?" He stroked her back lightly.

"They're nice women. But we don't have much in common."

"How so?"

"Well, they're all really feminine. Gracie's pregnant and glowing. Olivia already has a daughter, and she's a wonderful mom. Gillian teaches little children and loves them. And Ariel…well, *People* magazine voted her the sweetest and most appealing woman on the silver screen."

"I guess I'm missing something. Annalise, you're a knockout. Killer smile. Fabulous legs. And a personal style that I'd lay money lots of women try to emulate."

"And yet I've never had a serious boyfriend. Why do you think that is? I'll tell you," she said, rushing ahead before he could answer. "Men don't want someone like me. Well, I take that back. In bed, yes. Or as a trophy. They like the *outside* of me. But…"

"But what?"

She wriggled out of his loose embrace and scrubbed her hands over her face. He could almost see her withdrawing. "If I need a shrink, I'll pay for one," she said curtly. "I've got work to do, Sam. Do me a favor and get lost."

He felt his temper boil, despite the fact that he knew she was goading him deliberately. He had gotten too close, and she had reverted to her usual antagonistic ways.

"Fine," he said, feeling a real urge to throttle her. "I've done what Gram asked me to. You know the plan. I'll stay out of your hair until the snow melts and I can get back to my real life. But this…" He seized the rickety ladder and threw it against the wall, feeling a surge of satisfaction when it splintered into a half-dozen pieces. "This is off limits. If you really need to get up high, you'll have to ask for my help. I know it will choke you, but that's the deal."

He stormed out of the room, slamming the door behind him with as much force as he could muster. Ordinarily when he was this infuriated, he'd go to the gym and lift weights or box with the bag. Anything to burn off steam. But instead, he was being tormented by an advanced case of cabin fever, exacerbated by lust.

What was he supposed to do with a woman who made him crazy in bed, and yet did the same thing the rest of the time in an entirely different, far more maddening way? No man wanted to work this hard for sex.

A flurry of work-related phone calls did nothing to calm him. Instead, he threw on some cold weather gear and went outside to shovel the front steps. After that chore was completed to his satisfaction, he started on the path to the barn until sheer exhaustion forced him to abandon the hopeless endeavor. The storm had dropped at least twelve inches of snow, and the biting wind had turned the top layer to an icy crust that was like chiseling stone.

At last, chest heaving with exertion, he returned to the house. As he walked inside and caught a lingering whiff of what could only be Annalise's signature fragrance, a brilliant plan bloomed in his brain.

His motives were murky, even in his own head. Was he trying to make her mad? Or was he hoping for something more? Annalise had agreed to have sex with him while they were snowed in at the farmhouse. What did it matter if they fought like cats and dogs in between?

Why did he care that guys had hurt her in the past? And why did he still wince when he remembered that he was the first man to break her heart? She'd made it clear that she was no longer interested in any kind of emotional connection between the two of them. Why couldn't he leave well enough alone?

He'd gotten laid twice already. That should be enough for any man indulging a passing fancy. Was it really necessary to play the valiant knight for a woman who so clearly didn't need a hero? Annalise, by her own admission, could take care of herself. She was driven and focused, and fiercely intelligent.

And she hated romance. He grinned as he walked toward the kitchen. She didn't cook. So any meal planning was up to him. He had just the plan to even the scales after

that bloodbath of a pool game. Annalise was sharp. But
he had an advantage when it came to food. He planned to
use every bit of it.

Eight

When Annalise stretched to work the kinks out of her back, it was almost five o'clock. Winter's dark had fallen despicably early, sending her spirits plummeting. She was a runner on occasion, not hard-core-marathon level, but for exercise and stress relief. At the moment, nothing sounded more wonderful.

Unfortunately, she was trapped. And even worse, with a man who made her question everything she knew about herself.

She owed him an apology. The truth stuck in her throat, a huge lump of dismay wrapped in shame. Sam Ely was a nice guy. There. She admitted it. And he'd been doing his best to be kind and understanding when she uncharacteristically unburdened her soul.

But in return for his gentle, nonjudgmental listening, she'd been bitchy and ungrateful. No wonder he'd heaved a ladder across the room. Why did she have to be so touchy?

Her life would be a lot easier if she had ever learned to be open to people, to meet them halfway. But she'd grown up in such an environment of mistrust when it came to the outside world, it was hard to change her ways.

She ducked into her bedroom to freshen up. Even with the heat running, the house seemed chilly now that the sun had gone down. She untied her cardigan from around her neck and slipped her arms into the sleeves. Taking down her hair to brush out the dust and tangles, her hands shook suddenly as she remembered Sam in this room. In her bed. How would she ever sleep tonight? The image of his big nude body dwarfing the old-fashioned bed would be impossible to forget.

She had intended to tuck her long unruly hair back into its hair band at the nape of her neck, but feeling both foolish and hopeful, she left it loose. Looking in the mirror, she winced. With her hair tumbled around her shoulders, she looked far more feminine. And vulnerable. Neither of those were comfortable attributes as far as she was concerned.

When the growling of her stomach drove her to seek out sustenance, she decided she could hide no longer. Gathering her courage, she went in search of Sam.

The smells from the kitchen took her by surprise, making her mouth water and her nose twitch appreciatively. Gingerly, she pushed open the door.

Her host looked up, spatula in hand. When he was out of the room, she could almost convince herself that he was just another guy. But face-to-face… Her heart stuttered and then picked up its normal rhythm. He was almost too much to handle.

She swallowed and bit her lower lip, hovering in the doorway. "Something smells amazing," she said, offering an unspoken apology in hopes he would hear it and let her off the hook.

"It's just about ready," he said, his voice neutral. "How about opening that bottle of wine for us? And bring the glasses."

She did as he asked, ridiculously grateful that he wasn't frowning at her. Her nerves were jittery and her stomach unsettled. Though she deserved his censure, perhaps, she was emotional and broody, feeling more like an adolescent girl than a grown woman.

He finished dishing up two plates of pork chops, risotto and home-canned green beans while Annalise watched. Adding a slice of homemade bread to each, he picked up one plate in each hand and nodded his head. "I'll let you go first. We're going to eat in the living room."

She grabbed the crystal and the wine and bumped open the door to the adjoining room with her hip. When she saw what was on the other side, she stopped dead. From the sound of his muttered curse, Sam almost plowed into her from behind.

"Is there a problem?" he asked, his breath brushing her ear.

She swallowed hard, remembering her intent to be conciliatory. "Not at all."

The room was like a movie set. Sam had dragged a small table in front of the hearth and had stoked the fire until it burned merrily, chasing away the cold and cheering the atmosphere immeasurably. He had raided his grandmother's stash of antiques and farm-chic décor. A lace tablecloth set the stage for the brick-red earthenware plates he carried. An old Chianti bottle held a single beeswax candle.

Just behind the table, Sam had positioned the sofa and chairs close enough for post-dinner conversation. Even he couldn't roust up fresh flowers under the circumstances, but he had located a dried nosegay of lavender and heather and tucked it into a squatty china vase.

She set the glasses on the table so he wouldn't hear them rattle against one another. "This looks nice." Clearly, he was making a point. She had professed to dislike romantic gestures. Sam was calling her bluff.

He gently set down the plates and then poured the wine. "Sit and eat," he said, placing a glass filled almost to the brim with Chardonnay at her elbow. "Before it gets cold."

She obeyed reluctantly, feeling her heart race. This wasn't what she had signed on for. She didn't want Sam to be sweet and nice. She didn't want cozy evenings that would make her life feel incomplete when he was gone.

Sam, apparently oblivious to her consternation, dug into his food with the gusto of a hungry man enjoying his dinner. In between bites, he carried on a mostly one-sided conversation in which Annalise mumbled answers only when necessary.

She was fluent in three languages, had dined in four-star restaurants on as many continents and knew the intricacies of cutlery and wine pairings, but on this particular occasion, she was abashed to the point of social ineptitude.

Even Sam, determined to have a pleasant meal, eventually had to address her lack of conviviality. "Cat got your tongue?" he asked, lifting a sardonic eyebrow.

Annalise swallowed. "You've gone to a lot of trouble." Unfortunately, that statement came out sounding far more accusatory than appreciative.

"Don't worry, my little thornbush. This was for my benefit, not yours."

How did one go about calling a man a liar when an earnest apology was already in order? "Meaning what?"

"I was in a bad mood. We have cabin fever. I thought a semblance of civilization might be in order."

"I didn't think you were ever in a bad mood. At least when you're not with me," she amended hastily. "The society editor of the Charlottesville newspaper called you 'Virginia's Consummate Gentleman.'"

He lifted his glass to his lips, eyed her over the brim and drank deeply, the muscles in his throat flexing slightly. The flannel shirt had disappeared. Now he wore a pale blue dress shirt with an open collar and the sleeves rolled up. *Country* Sam was genial and approachable. This recent version, more like the man she knew in the city, was infinitely dangerous.

Twirling the stem of the glass between his fingers, he cocked his head and eyed her reflectively. "Since when do you follow the society columns? I thought Wolffs objected to such journalism on principle."

She stabbed the last bite of her tender pork and waved it at him. "I don't live in a cave. You're quite the celebrity in our corner of the world. I'm sure women line up in droves to be the next flavor of the month."

"Be fair," he said, his eyes narrowing. "I don't flit from flower to flower."

True, damn his hide. She wanted to take potshots at him, wanted it rather badly. But it wasn't that easy to do. He was damned near perfect. "Well, you sure don't show any signs of settling down. Or is all that talk about having kids just a ruse to lure softhearted romantics into your bed?"

"Thank God you're not a romantic," he said grimly. "No telling what would happen."

A ripple of sensation skated down her spine. She had plenty of armor to ward off a lazy, affable Sam. But when he went all dark-eyed and irritated, something about him made her belly flip with feelings that were definitely not wise.

"Are you avoiding the question?" The bite in her words appeared to amuse him.

"Not at all. I don't make any secret of my intentions, but I'm not foolish enough to let a woman think I'm serious when I'm not."

"And you haven't been? Serious, I mean?"

He leaned back in his chair. "Jealous, Annalise?"

She choked on her wine. "Of course not. We'd be a dreadful couple."

"Didn't seem like it last night…or this morning. When you were screaming my name."

Her face turned hot. "Sexual compatibility is nothing more than a fluke of hormones. The only reason I agreed to this temporary arrangement was that I've had a bit of a dry spell."

"How dry?" he shot back.

"None of your business."

"Hmm…"

He seemed to have the terrifying capability of seeing inside her brain. Could he really know how long she had carried a torch for him? She would die of humiliation if he realized.

Sam Ely had rejected her, rather vehemently, a long time ago. Never mind that her heartfelt declaration of love still rang in her ears with sick embarrassment. He had told her she was too young, too forward, too blatant in her pursuit.

Surely he gave her credit for having matured in the meantime.

She gazed into the fire, anything to avoid his laserlike gaze. "Shall I take care of the dishes?"

Sam stood, gathering their plates. "Don't move. Dessert is on the way."

When he left the room, she dropped her head in her hands, only to jerk upright moments later when he returned carrying two bowls of vanilla ice cream topped with strawberries.

At her look of surprise, Sam grinned. "Gram freezes dozens of quarts every summer." He had topped each serving with an artistic swirl of whipped cream. "Enjoy," he said.

She picked up her dessert spoon reluctantly. It was just ice cream. Nothing sexual about that. No reason for her palms to sweat and her pulse to do the cha-cha.

After all, strawberries conjured up the memories of long, hot summer afternoons. And happy times. Her childhood on Wolff Mountain had been idyllic in the beginning. When she was too young to know she was being held captive by her father's fears.

Almost as if Sam could hear her thoughts, he tapped the side of his bowl with the spoon. "Earth to Annalise. Where did you go?"

She licked a drop of melting ice cream from her upper lip. "I was thinking about being a kid. How wild and free it was."

"I envied you your spot on Wolff Mountain. You wouldn't remember this…because you were probably only five or six years old when it happened, but your brothers took me skinny-dipping in the creek one afternoon. You were the lookout. But you fell asleep, and your dad and uncle and my dad found us. They read us the riot act, because we had involved you in our escapade."

"My father was and is very protective of me."

"Which makes what we're doing pretty risky."

She frowned. "I'm not five years old anymore. I don't live on the mountain. My life is my own."

"You're telling me the Wolff men don't keep an eye on you?"

She wanted to be able to say no, but what was the point?

Sam knew too much about her family. "We all maintain the fiction that I come and go as I please. But yes. I realize that very little I do is completely private."

"And yet you mentioned building your own house on the mountain."

She grinned. "It *is* a conundrum, isn't it?"

"What do you want it to look like? The house, I mean."

"I don't honestly know. I have this hazy image of a screened-in back porch and wicker furniture where I can sit and watch the rain. As far as the house, I haven't nailed down any particular style. But I would want it to be peaceful and uncluttered. A place I could use as a retreat."

"And kid-friendly?"

Unease skittered along her nerve endings. "Maybe a few toys for the nieces and nephews. Perhaps a bunk bed."

"You honestly have no plans to be a mom one day?"

"None," she said flatly. She shoved the bowl aside, though she had eaten less than half of the dessert. "What about you? Are you going to turn your bachelor pad into a baby-proof garret?"

He shrugged. "Doubtful. And I'm not a fan of commuting, so this farmhouse will probably be used for weekends and holidays and a summer getaway. I'm thinking of building a family-sized house just outside of Charlottesville. I've been looking for the right parcel of land for the last couple of years."

"I see." Her dinner sat like lead in her stomach. When Sam didn't say anything more, the silence became oppressive. She struggled to change the subject. "I've ordered a lot of things already. If the weather cooperates, I imagine deliveries will begin to arrive Monday afternoon. I'll start painting a room at a time."

"We can hire people to do that," he said, a tiny line

forming between his brows. "Gram is paying for your expertise, not your muscle."

"I'm picky," Annalise admitted. No point hiding it. "And a bit of a control freak. I'd rather know the work is being done right."

"Then order a ladder," he groused. "I'm not paying for any trips to the emergency room."

Suddenly their earlier fight was the elephant in the room. Not for anything would she admit that his temper had surprised and intrigued her. It indicated a level of emotional involvement that seemed uncharacteristic of a man who managed to make everything in his life look easy and charmed.

Annalise tensed. Almost without knowing it, she had been lulled into a sense of complacency by the good food, Sam's innocuous conversation and the blazing fire. Escape seemed the smart course. "If you won't let me help with the dishes," she said, "I think I'll turn in for the night. I'm reading a good book."

Sam reached across the table and gripped one of her wrists in his big hand. "No."

"Excuse me?" Surely his caveman technique wasn't the reason butterflies tumbled in her chest.

He got up, drawing her to her feet, as well. "I have plans for the evening," he said mildly, although the look in his eyes was anything but. Sexual tension prowled like a dark shadow in the room. "You can cooperate, or I'll persuade you."

"My God, you're an arrogant ass." They were standing so close together she could see a tiny scar on his right cheekbone. His body radiated heat and a scent that was all male. Equal parts soap and sexual determination.

"And you're an aggravating shrew," he said, his gaze on her parted lips. "Lord knows why I want you."

"And yet here we are."

"Indeed." He wrapped a strand of her hair around his finger. "Why do you think that is?"

"You're bored?"

"Not in the least."

"I strike you as some kind of challenge?"

"Like what?"

"I don't know," she said, twisting away to stand in front of the fire. "Maybe you have some deep-seated need to prove you're irresistible."

"I've been rejected on occasion, Annalise. Trust me."

There it was. That tricky word. *Trust.* "What exactly do you want from me?"

"You promised me this weekend. Until the snow melts. I propose we call a truce. Enjoy tonight and tomorrow. And then Monday morning you can decide if you want me to leave. Without you."

"Of course I do. Why would you stay? You'd only get in my way."

He stalked her, backing her toward the corner where the hearth met the alcove. With a flick of his wrist, he reached for the light switch and plunged the room into semidarkness, illumined only by the fire and the single candle. "A truce means you have to pretend you like me."

Her butt smacked into the wall. "I'm not that good an actress."

He grinned, his teeth flashing like a rogue pirate. "You're a spoiled brat, Princess."

"You're a bossy, high-handed pig."

"Kiss me."

The rough command took the starch out of her knees. Her hands flattened on the surface behind her. "I won't."

His arms bracketed her shoulders as his head lowered. "Liar, liar…"

What happened next was like every romantic chick flick she'd ever seen all rolled into one. She was pretty sure an orchestra played somewhere in the background. And Sam's warm, firm lips put any one of a number of leading men to shame as he moved in, surrounded her and took what he wanted. *Oh, Lordy.*

Somehow her arms ended up around his neck, her breasts mashed up against a rock-hard chest. He tasted like sweet berries and cream. The roughness of his tongue tantalized as he intruded ever so gently between lips that trembled. She barely had time to catch her breath before he scooped her into his arms and pressed her against the wall. "You are so damned hot," he said.

"I drive you insane."

He bit the side of her neck. "But I like it."

She giggled. She actually giggled. And that was when she knew she was in trouble. Because Annalise Wolff never giggled. "We already had sex once today." As excuses went, it was pretty pitiful.

Sam snorted. "Then we're way behind."

He hefted her by the ass and skirted the table, knocking over a chair in his haste. She would have giggled again if she had been able to force air from her throat.

Something was strangling her, some desperate, aching realization that her life was never going to be the same after this weekend. "I'm not very good at it," she blurted out, not wanting to pretend with him.

"At what?" He dumped her on the sofa and kneeled beside her to unzip her pants.

"Sex," she moaned, feeling his fingers slip beneath the lacy edge of her panties.

Sam's eyes blazed with hunger, his cheekbones slashed with dark color. "Could have fooled me. Shut up, Princess. Unless you want to say something sensible."

He dragged off her pants, underwear and shoes in one reckless maneuver. Next her sweater, shirt and bra went flying. He opened his jeans and came down between her legs. The denim abraded her inner thighs as he found what he wanted.

"There's no room," she panted. The narrow sofa wasn't made for sexual activity.

"I'll make room." His voice was rough with determination. "Damn, you're wet," he groaned as he tested her readiness with two fingers. The scrape of his fingernail on her delicate flesh sent a keening cry echoing toward the ceiling. But when Sam entered her fully and pushed his way home, the simultaneous cessation of breathing, his and hers, lent magic to the connection.

Five seconds passed. Then ten. She lifted her hips, begging wordlessly. Sam kissed her gently, his mouth firm and sweet. "What is it you do to me?"

Annalise wrapped her legs around his waist. He filled her deliciously. "It's all you," she said, eyes closed with bliss. "I'll hate myself later for saying this, but damn, you're good."

"No cussing, remember?"

He moved his hips, driving deeper. Pinball flashes of pleasure coalesced and ignited at the point where their bodies joined. "Please, please, please," she whispered, voice hoarse, lungs barely able to function.

"Annalise…" His gruff shout sent her over the edge as he hit his own wall, his release coming in a rapid, forceful finish that left her weak and clinging to him like he was the only steady rock in a swirling current.

As their breathing slowed, she became aware of the fact that Sam was heavy, really heavy. And his shirt buttons were making permanent tattoos on her breasts. "Air," she muttered. "I need air."

"Sorry." With patent reluctance, Sam lifted his body off hers and stumbled to his feet.

Suddenly, her nudity in the face of his fully clothed state made her blush. "Will you hand me my shirt and pants, please?"

"No." Again that single, macho negative. Any moment now, she should protest. Instead, she wrapped her arms across her breasts and curled on her side, hiding things he had already seen. "I need my clothes," she said, scrupulously polite.

He threw a couple more logs on the fire and turned to face her. "We're not finished." He shrugged out of his shirt. "I'm just getting started." The sight of his beautiful, masculine chest made her tremble, despite the fact that he had so recently satisfied her. Sam looked different in this light. Like a Viking plunderer...or a wild-eyed barbarian.

It occurred to her that she should show at least a modicum of spunk. Instead of letting him run the show. "What if I object?" Fat chance.

He shrugged, muscles rippling in his arms and torso. "You won't. I promise. Come here, baby."

Nine

Sam had barely touched his wine, yet his head was spinning. The incredible climax he'd experienced moments ago was already fading into the distance, obscured by an urgent need to take her again.

He was not himself. It wasn't false modesty to say he was good at satisfying women sexually. He'd received numerous breathless accolades over the years. But holy hell, the nuclear explosion that triggered when he and Annalise connected was incredible.

At the moment, she was soft, satiated, approachable. It was rapidly becoming apparent to him that the only time he could truly reach her, without the barrier of acerbity she used as a shield, was during sex. When she forgot that she was mad at him…when she forgot that she held a long-standing grudge.

Post-orgasmic amnesia. That's what he should call it. Maybe he had discovered something never before known to science. In another twenty minutes she'd be scowling at him. So the secret was—keep her naked and underneath him. Or on top, or…

As he shed his pants, shoes and socks, his sex reared to attention in increments. Annalise's eyes widened when she took note. He grinned, holding out his hand. "I said, come here."

She stood up, naked and lovely and so very tempting. He knew in his gut that she was right about the two of them. A relationship doomed from the start could only end in messy collateral damage. They weren't living in a vacuum. Their families had been friends for three decades. Whether they liked it or not, their worlds were intertwined.

Which meant that a train wreck on the road to intimacy would affect more than just the two of them.

For a brief moment, he entertained the idea of permanence. He was tired of playing the field. Annalise was smart and beautiful and entertaining both in and out of bed. But she didn't want children. And sadly, that was a deal-breaker for him. Besides, he needed a wife someday who would look at him with adoration, one who believed in romance. Not a termagant who made him want to hide the kitchen knives.

She reached down and took him in her hand, squeezing gently. "I thought you were an old man. It seems I was wrong."

His skin tightened in gooseflesh all over his body. At the moment, babies were the last things on his mind. He closed his eyes, hands fisted at his hips as she caressed the hot length of him. Her fingers curled carefully around his balls, playing with them, testing their weight.

He tried to speak, swallowed hard and tried again. "I have an idea." It had been on his mind ever since that morning when she sat on the edge of the bed, back turned

toward him, and he saw the way her slim shoulders and
narrow waist flared into a heart-shaped bottom. "Give
me a sec."

She frowned when he escaped her light hold. "I'm getting cold."

"Not for long." Grabbing one of the quilts they had used
during the night, he folded it carefully and laid it over the
wooden arm of the sofa. He snagged her wrist. "That last
time was too fast. I want to try slow and easy."

Her eyes widened. "I don't do kinky."

He shrugged, trying to suppress a grin...and failing.
"How do you know?"

Her teeth worried her bottom lip. But her raspberry nipples puckered into hard nubs. He brushed them with his
thumbs. Annalise shut her eyes, almost as if she couldn't
bear to watch.

"I'll repeat the question, darlin', how do you know?"

She swayed toward him, her body lissome and compliant. "I just know. Why did you give me so much wine?"
she complained, her arms curling around his neck. "I can't
think straight."

"Oh, no, no, no," he said, disentangling himself and
holding her at arm's length. "I'm not going to let you blame
this craziness on alcohol-induced bad judgment. We're
going into this eyes wide open. It's a choice, Annalise.
Tell me you want me."

She licked her lips. He was damn sure she had no idea
how erotically beautiful she looked. Or how confused. It
was the uncertainty in her gaze that slowed him down.
"Or tell me you don't want me," he amended, releasing
her abruptly and stepping back. "But I won't be accused of
taking advantage of you. If you really want to stop, we'll
pretend like none of this ever happened."

She shivered hard, as if a ghost had brushed her shoulder. "I *want* you," she said, the words little more than a whisper. "But I know I shouldn't."

He flinched inwardly. He didn't want to be any woman's guilty pleasure, much less Annalise's. "Well, that's honest, at least."

"I hurt your feelings. I didn't mean to."

"I suppose you thought I didn't have any."

She frowned. "Nothing ever seems to bother you."

"You'd be surprised." The ache in his chest was a mixture of arousal and disappointment and a soupçon of Annalise's confusion. God knows, this wasn't what he'd imagined when he drove out to the farm for the weekend. If anything he been dreading a couple of days of armed hostilities as he carried out his grandmother's request to help Annalise settle in.

"Why do you want to have sex with me?"

He rubbed his forehead with the heels of his hands. "Why do women need to have everything analyzed in advance? I just do." He paused, his turn to frown. "Why wouldn't I?"

"I don't know. I've seen the women you date. None of them have much in common with me."

"I can't believe two naked people are standing here having this inane discussion. Only you, Annalise. Suffice it to say that you turn me on. End of story."

"You're getting angry."

"No. I'm getting frustrated. There's a difference. I'll ask you one last time. Do you want me?"

The length of the pause in the conversation was long enough to accommodate an entire symphony…or so it seemed. But at last, she moved, she nodded. A smile would have made him feel better, but at this moment, he wasn't inclined to be picky. "Is that a yes?"

She held out her hand. "It is. I'll never accuse you of anything, Sam. You're an honorable guy. I know that."

Her praise irritated him. "I'm no better or worse than any other man. But I will do my best not to hurt you again. Once in a lifetime was enough."

She managed a small, hesitant smile. "That seems fair."

Feeling his heart thudding against his ribs, he took the hand she offered and drew her into his embrace. "Your skin is like ice," he exclaimed, rubbing his hands up and down her arms. "Come toward the fire for a minute." He faced her toward the flames and stood behind her, wrapping his arms around her beneath her breasts. His erection nestled in the cleft of her bottom. Fine tremors in his limbs reminded him that a baser part of him wanted more than this. But he ignored the insistent pulse of arousal and buried his face in her hair.

She rested her head against his shoulder, her fingers linking with his. "You play dirty," she said, drowsiness in her posture and her voice.

"How so?"

"Romance. It's filled the room. I'm tripping over it." She chuckled. "Maybe it's not so bad after all."

"I'm glad you approve. Are you warmer?" he asked hopefully, about to lose the battle with the constraints he'd placed on his desperate need.

She turned suddenly, taken by surprise. "According to you, I'm hot." Her hands settled on his shoulders and she reached up on tiptoe and gave him a sweet kiss that had a kick to it. "Let's see how kinky you can be."

He'd been hard for so long it was a miracle his brain functioned at all. "We'll start small," he promised, leading her back to the sofa.

With a smile that would have brought any man to his

knees, she brushed his shaft. "Wrong choice of words, Mr. Ely. Not small at all."

Her laughter warmed him from the inside out. If nothing else, he would be grateful that this weekend had eased the pain from the past. He didn't wanted to be at odds with Annalise Wolff. He wanted to be her friend, her very intimate friend.

Without asking for permission, he bent her over the fluffy quilt. The height of the sofa arm was perfect. And as he had suspected, her pert bottom was a sight to see, presented in this position.

"What do you want me to do with my hands?" Her voice was muffled by her hair.

He scooped the thick tresses over her right shoulder so he could see her face. "I'll take care of that." He pulled her arms behind her back and held her wrists. With his other hand, he widened the stance of her legs and reached between her thighs to stroke gently.

Annalise gave a soft exclamation that could have meant any number of things. Her eyes were closed, her face turned toward the fire. He separated the plump folds of her sex and felt the slick moisture that readied her body for his.

It shocked him to realize that his hands were shaking. Badly. Was it arousal or the fear of messing this up? He wanted to show her how sexy she was, how desirable, how perfectly feminine in every way. If later, she chose to take the lead, he had no problem with that. In fact, the thought of Annalise Wolff dominating him in the bedroom had a certain skin-tightening charm.

But he sensed that at the moment she wanted to capitulate, to submit, to revel in the freedom of her sex. To experience the power of driving a man to the point of insanity.

In truth, Sam was almost there.

He fit the head of his shaft to her passage and teased

her with it. She squirmed. Her face was flushed. At least the part he could see. Wondering if she would consent to play with him, he decided to test the waters. "I'm going to release your wrists," he said gruffly. "I want you to stretch your arms over your head, link your hands, and rest them on the sofa. Do you understand?"

"Yes." The low, slurred tenor of her reply tapped in him a primal response.

"Then do it." When he let go of her wrists, she obeyed his command.

The vision of Annalise stretched out in front of him like an offering seared his brain…so vivid, he could see it even when he closed his eyes and sucked in a shaky breath. With both of his hands now free, he caressed her butt. Her ass was pale as the moon, curvaceous, perfectly proportioned to her healthy body.

A small mole, high on her right hip, fascinated him. When he bent and kissed the tiny beauty mark, Annalise sighed deeply. Once again, he positioned himself for entry. "You were beautiful as a teenager," he whispered, fearful of bringing up the past, though beyond dissimulation. "But now you take my breath away. I want you. I'm going to have you. Again and again until you beg me to stop. You've bewitched me, seduced me, destroyed me."

Slowly, he pushed into her, painfully stimulated by the angle of penetration and the caveman position. He wasn't even sure if this was for him or for her. The fit was tight, her body squeezing his until his skin dampened and his eyes stung with the sheer pleasure of it.

"Talk to me," he begged. "Tell me what you want."

She glanced over her shoulder, a sultry, sirenlike gaze. "Whatever you have to give me, Sam. I want it all."

He drove into her again and again. First slow, then fast, then slow again. His fingers splayed on her ass, plumping, caressing. "I wish you could see yourself right now. God, you're amazing."

She arched her back, and reared up on her elbows, forehead resting on her clenched hands. "More. Don't stop."

He reached beneath her and caressed the spot where her pleasure centered. Annalise jerked and moaned. Timing the stroke of his finger to the slide of his shaft, he took them both to the edge and hovered there. "Do you want to come?"

She said a word that once again destroyed her resolution.

Sam chuckled, but it was a breathless, weak sound. The air in his lungs had evaporated. Suddenly, his control snapped, and with a groan, he pushed all the way to the core of her and pumped recklessly as he gripped her hips and emptied himself into the warm welcome of his unlikely lover.

Hours later, he rolled over and glanced at the clock. Annalise was in *his* bed this time, in the room that was his whenever his visited his grandparents. The comfortable king mattress accommodated his lanky frame. He held her close, relishing the sweet, trusting way she rested in his embrace.

They had made love for hours, finally abandoning the living room and coming upstairs to collapse into bed. Sighing deeply with repletion and contentment, he succumbed once again to the warm embrace of much-needed sleep.

When he opened his eyes the second time, Annalise was gone. The stone of disappointment that crushed his chest was enormous. Yesterday morning, he had understood her need to flee. But last night he thought they had forged a tenuous understanding, a fledgling truce.

His mouth was fuzzy and his head ached. Reluctantly,

he dialed back his expectations for the remainder of the
weekend. Annalise was not like other women. And there
was absolutely no way to predict her reactions from one
minute to the next.

Perhaps all she wanted from him was sex. For any other
guy at any other moment, that would have been a pretty
sweet deal. But Sam and Annalise had a past, a connection, an undeniable chemistry. The potential was there to
create something wonderful.

He was beginning, however, to have a sinking suspicion that she was determined never to let that happen.
Was it because he had rejected her once upon a time? Or
did he simply not want anything more from him than one
naughty weekend?

Annalise hummed as she worked, her body aching
pleasantly, and her cheeks heating as she relived each moment of the incredible night before. Sam Ely was a genius.
Even with her limited experience, it was evident that he
had devoted a lot of time to learning about women.

Perhaps she should have been jealous. His sexual expertise was no doubt the product of many intimate liai-
sons. But oddly, she didn't begrudge any of those women
their momentary connections to Sam. He wasn't *with* any
of those women now. He had moved on.

Despite the painful experience in the past when she
threw herself at him and suffered an ignominious rejection, she and Sam had known each other for a very long
time. They had a relationship. It might not be the stuff of
romantic fiction, but it was something. Even if this weekend turned out to be all she ever had of him in a sexual
way, the tentative resurrection of their friendship would
be enough.

The essence of that thought rang false, but she ignored

the warning signs. Sam wasn't hers to keep. He deserved someone who wanted the things he wanted. A woman who could create a home and a family with him. Annalise was unable to do either of those things. There were still secrets between them. But that was okay. Because after this weekend, they would be something they hadn't been in many years. Friends.

She pulled out her laptop and perched on a stool in the downstairs room Sam's grandmother had used as a sewing nook. Colors and patterns buzzed in her head, each jockeying for favor. This was her favorite part of the job... choosing palettes, accents, lighting. Already she was falling in love with the farmhouse.

Sam was right. It was too far from the city to be practical as a main residence, but how wonderful it would be to get away on a warm spring weekend, a lazy summer month in August, a crisp, colorful autumn retreat. She could almost see the children playing outside, hear their high-pitched laughter.

Several ancient oaks provided the perfect spot for tire swings. In summer, the generous shade would accommodate impromptu picnics, as well. And the house was big enough for lots of company. Even the burgeoning Wolff clan.

That thought brought her up short. Surely she wasn't weaving improbable daydreams about her and Sam. She hadn't been lying when she told him she didn't really like romance. Romance was what had led her to throw herself at him when she was twenty-one.

Romance made people stupid, and Annalise was not stupid. Besides, even if by some miracle she and Sam fell in love and managed not to drive each other nuts, the truth remained. She was not wife material.

His long-ago words still rang in her ears: *Men like gen-*

tle, feminine women…soft, self-effacing. Perhaps he hadn't really meant that. He said he'd been trying to let her down easy and keep her from doing something stupid with another man who might have accepted her artless invitation and tossed her aside afterward.

But even so, he'd said the words out loud, and their power lingered. Annalise wouldn't change herself even if she could. She liked who she was. But she had to accept that there were some things her upbringing had cost her. And having a family was one of those.

"There you are. Have you had breakfast?"

Sam's voice startled her so badly she nearly dropped her computer. She closed it and stood, clutching it to her chest like armor. "I had some toast and coffee."

"Did you sleep well?" His topaz and chocolate eyes searched her face, his sculpted mouth unsmiling.

She squirmed inwardly. "Yes, thank you." Good Lord. This was a man who had seen her naked, who had done exquisitely intimate things to her and with her. Why was the aftermath so damned difficult?

He lounged in the doorway, his hands shoved in the pockets of faded jeans. Another flannel shirt, this one gold with a navy windowpane pattern, strained across his broad shoulders. His eyelids drooped and his hair was mussed. He looked like a man who had been up all night.

Her prim response amused him. His lips quirked, and he cocked his head, studying her with an intensity that seemed to strip the clothes from her body. "I think we need some exercise."

The color in her face deepened as her thighs clenched. "Well, I…uh…"

"Outside," Sam clarified. "In the fresh air. The temperature has come up considerably. Gram and Pops have all sorts of winter gear in the mudroom. How about it?"

She glanced out the window to the world of white. Suddenly, nothing sounded more appealing. "I'd like that."

In twenty minutes they were bundled up in layers of warm clothing. Fortunately for Annalise, Gram had left behind a pair of yellow galoshes that were close enough to the right size to keep her feet warm and dry.

The first bite of cold air as they stepped outside took her breath away, but when they rounded the house to the side sheltered from the wind, where Sam had scraped a partial path, it wasn't bad at all. The sun shone down valiantly, doing its best to melt the snow. Annalise lifted her face to the sky and inhaled the smell of wood smoke drifting from the chimney.

The farm was somnolent, like Sleeping Beauty's castle. Sam's grandparents had sold off all the livestock years ago when they decided they no longer wanted the responsibility of actually running a dairy farm. Any farmhands had long since been let go. Though the barn was in good shape and the outbuildings were sturdy, the place was a ghost town. Only the house itself showed any signs of life.

Annalise turned to Sam. "Do you think you'll ever turn this back into a working farm? You've talked about how much you loved it as a kid. It seems a shame to use only the house."

He shaded his eyes with one hand and looked out across the fields that had once supported acres of corn and herds of cows. "I'll bring the horses back, at some point. And maybe lease the land so it will be producing as it should. But I doubt the farm will ever be what it once was. Unless one of *my* children takes an interest in agriculture."

The way he said the word *children* hurt something deep in her chest. "How many do you want? Kids, I mean."

He shrugged. "That will depend on my wife, I guess. But at least three. Maybe four."

Four? Annalise felt faint.

When she was silent, he continued. "I have the means to support a big family. And I want a noisy house, not like where I grew up. By the time I was eleven, Mom quit making me go to a babysitter after school. I got off the bus and let myself in with a key we kept hidden under a rock in the backyard. She always left me snacks ready…lemonade in the fridge, fresh fruit and cookies. But I hated the silence when I went inside."

He visibly shrugged off his preoccupation with the past. "I don't want you to think it was a terrible childhood, 'cause it wasn't. My mom is a great person, and she did the best she could with a rambunctious son who was pretty mischievous. I had plenty of friends in the neighborhood. So I spent a lot of time at their houses."

"Tell me something, Sam," she said, touched with compassion by the picture he painted. "How can you be so sure you won't end up divorced like your parents? The statistics aren't in your favor."

He picked up a stick and hurled it into the distance, an almost palpable sense of frustration in the jerky motion. "For one thing, I've learned the difference between lust and love. And how important compatibility is. That's where people go wrong when they marry too young. They ignore the fact that attraction and wild sex are not a sound basis for long-term commitment. I guess I can't be one-hundred-percent certain, but the reason I've waited this long to get married is so I can be sure of as many variables as possible."

"Sure how?" Annalise kicked at a stone with her boot. This was an odd place for a serious conversation, but at least out here they weren't likely to strip off their clothes and attack each other. Just the thought of it made her layers of clothing far too warm.

"My parents weren't a great match from the beginning. I'm going to pick someone who shares my values, who wants what I want."

"No offense, Sam, but you said that your dad's workaholic nature was partly to blame for the divorce. Aren't you like him in that way?" She wasn't being mean. It was a fair question.

He unzipped his coat partway, pulled the hood back and ran his hands through his hair. In the bright sun she could see glints of red in his thick chestnut waves. "It's true," he said. "I work long hours. But that's because I can. If I had a wife and kids at home, things would be different."

"Mmm…"

His eyes snapped with displeasure. "You don't believe me?"

"I think you're pretty set in your ways. Are you expecting this paragon of a wife to stay home with the kids?"

"I hope she'll want to…since finances won't be an issue. The two of us will share responsibility for child-rearing, but it seems to work best when one parent stays home to give the kids security."

She couldn't argue with that. Her mother had not been around, and her dad, though she loved him dearly, wasn't the cuddly type. The Norman Rockwell existence Sam described was very appealing. As long as he acknowledged that his wife would surely have dreams outside of simply being a mother. Somehow, she thought he would. Despite any evidence to the contrary, Sam was not a chauvinist.

"Well," she said, feeling depression settle like a pall over the day, "I wish you luck." Any last glimmer of hope that Sam might care for her in a deeper sense withered and died. The two of them were not compatible. They fought like cats and dogs. She'd be a lousy mother. Even if she were willing to put her career on hold and give him multiple babies, the picture would fall apart rapidly.

When he wasn't looking, she scooped up a handful of snow and shaped it into a ball. Pool wasn't the only game she knew how to play. She wandered a few yards away, ostensibly to look at an old doghouse covered in snow.

Sam was gazing up at the eaves of the farmhouse, probably wondering about things like dry rot and bats and other homeowner headaches. Taking careful aim, remembering everything her brothers had taught her, she reared back and flung the sphere of snow as hard as she could.

Thwack! It couldn't have been a more perfect bull's-eye. The snowball caught the side of Sam's neck, disintegrated from the force of the hit and slid messily into the open collar of his shirt.

"Hey," he shouted indignantly. "No fair."

The childhood rejoinder made her grin. "You're the one who said we needed exercise." Rapidly, she scooped up more handfuls of snow, creating her ammunition and using the doghouse as cover.

Sam's glare promised retribution. He amassed an arsenal as well, only instead of huddling behind a pitiful barrier like her abandoned pet shed, he stacked his snowballs on a windowsill and climbed up beside the house to stand on an old stump. Now he had the advantage of higher ground.

When he turned to put one last projectile on his growing pile, Annalise shot to her feet, threw three snowballs in quick succession and crowed when every one of them hit the intended target. Sam's hair was coated in white, and he had to wipe snow from his mouth.

Revenge was swift and targeted. Too late, she remembered that Sam had pitched for his college baseball team. A hailstorm of snowballs descended on top of her, ricocheting off the roof, the walls and the corners of her shelter. At least half of the shots arced perfectly over the small building and landed smack on her head. She huddled into her coat, pulled the hood down tight and waited him out.

Inevitably, he ran out of ammo. Now it was her turn. Standing with impunity, she mimicked his blitzkrieg, pelting him unmercifully. This time she played dirty, aiming for his masculinity. The snow was too wet and she was too far away to do any real damage, but watching Sam hop and curse and try not to fall off the stump had her laughing until tears ran down her face.

Unfortunately, she, too, eventually ran out of steam and snowballs. Ducking back down, her heart pounding, she waited for the answering volley. Nothing happened. Surely he had managed to make a new pile of ammo by now. Dead silence reigned, broken only by the faraway raucous cry of a crow.

What was happening? Why wasn't he firing back? Tentatively, she peeked around the corner of the doghouse, expecting any moment to be hit in the face with icy, wet snow.

The stump had been abandoned. No sign of Sam anywhere, though messy footprints led in all directions. Surely he wouldn't have gone back into the house without her. Inside her gloves, her fingers started to go numb. And the knees of her pants were getting wet. Where in the hell was he?

Without warning, snow crunched behind her and what felt like a shovelful of snow slithered down her back. She yelled in shock, flailing wildly and knocking Sam's head with hers in the process. He had made a wide circle, sneaking up behind her in a creditable ambush attack.

Before she could recover, he flipped her onto her back

and shoved more snow up under the front of her coat. "Stop, you big goof," she cried. "I'm freezing."

He unzipped her parka and massaged the snow into her chest. "I want to hear you cry uncle," he said, grinning evilly.

She tried to ignore the fact that her body was heading for hypothermia. Smiling sweetly to disarm him, she waited one click…two…and then kneed him dangerously close to the groin before rolling away, reversing their positions and landing on top of him with her forearm over his windpipe.

Sam's eyes crossed and he coughed out a weak imprecation. "I should have known better," he groaned. "Martial arts. Not Barbie dolls. Rookie mistake on my part."

Annalise knew he could overpower her. Despite her considerable skill, he outweighed her by at least seventy pounds. And he was strong and powerful. But for the moment, he allowed her a victory.

He held up a hand. "I surrender."

"Hah."

"You don't believe me?" His lifted eyebrow was all innocence.

She stood up and shivered as melted snow ran down her back and belly. "I don't trust you one tiny bit. You're a schemer and a conniver."

"Only in sports," he said gravely. "Not in real life."

She had been teasing him, nothing more, but his sudden, soft-spoken vow seemed to be aimed at communicating something significant. "Well, duh, I know that," she said. "Eagle Scout. Outstanding young alumnus, president of the United Way campaign. I suppose I'm the only person to ever leave the Sam Ely fan club. Right?"

He stood up and winced when he realized his entire

backside was covered in snow. Brushing himself off, and not even looking at her, he shrugged. "I was rather hoping you'd ask for a new membership card." When she didn't say anything, mainly because her heart had lodged uncomfortably in her throat, he faced her. "Or am I way off base? Do you still hate my guts?"

How had they gone from playful to deadly serious so quickly? The words she wanted to say trembled on her tongue. *I never stopped loving you, Sam.* But good Lord, she couldn't say that. And see the pity and compassion on his face? She'd rather go to her grave an old maid.

"I don't hate you," she said lightly. "But if I catch pneumonia, I hope your workmen's comp is all paid up."

Ten

Sam suffered the tsunami of disappointment stoically. What had he expected? A miracle in less than forty-eight hours? Annalise would never forgive him, not really. And he might as well give up on winning her approval. It was a lost cause.

Swallowing his bitter defeat, a battle she didn't even realize she had won, he waved a hand. "Let's go inside."

On the back porch, they stripped off their outerwear. "Leave it," Sam said. "I'll put it all in the dryer later." He watched her wring water from her hair, and that single, feminine motion made him hard. *What the hell,* he thought. If sex was all that worked between them, he might as well enjoy it. "We shouldn't traipse through the house all wet," he said calmly.

Annalise sat on a stool and tugged off her boots. "What would you suggest?" Her pants were soaked through, and her sweater was not much better.

"Strip naked," he said. "We'll make a dash for the shower."

Her eyes widened and two spots of color bloomed on her cheeks. "Naked?"

"It's the smart thing to do." Not waiting for her to follow his lead, he dragged his shirt over his head, shoved his sodden pants to his feet and stepped out of them. His socks were already balled up inside his boots. In spite of the frigid temperature, his sex reared eagerly, perhaps not at full mast, but headed that way.

When Annalise seemed literally frozen, he lent a hand, undressing her matter-of-factly, not lingering to caress her, or signal seduction in any way.

Now they both stood bare-skinned, their limbs covered in gooseflesh. "After you," he said quietly, unable to tear his gaze away from her nudity. He put a hand at the small of her back and urged her forward. "My shower's bigger. We'll go upstairs."

By the time they made it to his room, he couldn't feel his feet. And Annalise's lips were blue. Leaving her to stand on the bath mat for a moment, he leaned into the shower enclosure, adjusted the water to a warm, steady spray and linked his fingers with hers. "C'mon, honey. Let's get you warmed up."

She was so docile, he worried for a moment that she might actually be in danger of shock from the cold. But as soon as he got her under the steamy water, color returned to her skin, and she moaned in sheer pleasure. The sound she made went straight to the heart of his need, dragging him into insanity without a qualm.

When he stepped behind her, soaped up his hands and reached around to wash her breasts, she didn't make even a token protest. She stood mute, a lifelike statue, allowing him to shampoo her long, raven hair, to tip back her head beneath the water and rinse the bubbles away.

In that position, he couldn't help himself. He had to taste those puckered rosy nipples, his tongue circling them, suckling them one at a time. When her knees gave out, he supported her with one arm behind her back.

He reached for the soap and eased his way down between her legs. Lazily, he slid the wet bar over her sex, back and forth. Annalise came to life, panting, lifting a leg to steady herself against the shower wall.

Laughing softly, Sam dropped the soap and used his fingers to finish the job. She responded to him beautifully, lifting her hips into his touch, arching her neck as she reached for what he wanted to postpone. He wished that she felt comfortable enough with him to initiate sex, but that was asking a lot given their history.

He scraped her hair from her face, drawing it in his fist to the back of her neck. Even wet and bedraggled, she was stunning. He momentarily leaned his forehead against hers, still holding her by the hair. "I know from experience," he said, "that the water is going to run cold in about two minutes. How do you feel about moving this to the bedroom?"

His prosaic question seemed to snap her out of some trancelike state. Her jaw dropped, and she winced, as if only now realizing that she was cavorting with a naked man in the shower. "We've wasted a lot of time playing around. I need to be working."

He gaped at her, his temper rising. She was pretending that she could walk away. That their sexual intimacy meant nothing to her. In his gut, he didn't think she really believed that, but her attempt to shove him to a safe emotional distance infuriated him.

He jerked on the ponytail he had crafted, not hard

enough to hurt her...but with enough force to gain her attention. "Is this where I'm supposed to seduce you against your objections? What kind of game are you playing with me?"

"I'm not," she cried, tears welling in her eyes.

Her genuine distress nicked him. Tears from a woman who never showed weakness indicated a level of involvement that dared give him a flicker of hope. "You could have fooled me," he muttered, but the words held little heat.

She licked her lips, despite the fact that water still pelted down upon them. "I'm sorry if you think that. It's not true. I would never do such a thing, I swear. I know that whatever we're doing here isn't permanent, but you're important to me, Sam."

"Forget it." Now he felt guilty for his outburst. He shut off the water and grabbed two towels, handing her one without comment, using the other for himself. He turned his back, unable to watch the erotic image of his nemesis drying one slender limb at a time. He strode into the bedroom and stepped into a pair of knit boxers. "Do you want me to go downstairs and get you some clothes?" He raised his voice because she was still in the bathroom.

"There's a pair of pajamas and matching slippers in the top drawer of the dresser." The words were subdued. He heard cabinets opening, and then the sound of the hair dryer.

He shivered hard. It was a good thing Gram and Pops were getting the heat and air revamped. This old house was chilly in winter, even when the power *wasn't* out. The trip downstairs and back was accomplished in record time, mainly because he resisted the urge to rummage through the piles of sherbet-colored lingerie. The delicate garments held a faint fragrance that was uniquely Annalise. When he imagined her wearing them, confusion and hunger made him restless.

He took the stairs two at a time, stopping short when he entered the bedroom. She was standing in the doorway to the bathroom wearing one of his shirts she'd found hanging on a chair. Her legs were bare, her eyes huge with vulnerability, her hair mostly dry.

"Do you want to change into these?" he asked.

He saw her chest rise and fall. Her lower lip trembled. "No more pretending from me, Sam. I might as well be honest. What I *want* is to get in bed with you."

It was the most she had ever offered him. The tremulous words socked him in the gut, disarming him even as they aroused. He swallowed his pique and decided to be offended later. "Well, okay then." He dropped her clothing on a chair and approached her. "We're going to talk today…sometime. About why you and I have this weird, screwed-up relationship. But right now…" He scooped her up into his arms and carried her toward the bed.

"Right now, what?"

"Never mind," he sighed, not sure what he'd been about to say. She felt perfect in his arms. As if for the first time, he had found what he was looking for. But it didn't make any sense at all. Annalise was not the kind of woman he wanted for the long haul. She was sharp-tongued and opinionated and bossy. And though her body was sinfully soft, her personality was anything but.

She thrived on confrontation, and she'd rather best him at anything than give an inch. He was convinced that another Annalise lurked inside. A woman who didn't have a chip on her shoulder. A woman who could warm a man with her caring and her courage. But for whatever reason, she had decided to keep the walls in place.

She had granted Sam access to her body this weekend,

but the essence of who she was remained under lock and key. It saddened him, but he was not really in a position to challenge her on it. Not unless he was prepared to go forward with the relationship.

Tossing back the covers, he deposited her on the bed, coming down beside her and covering them both with the blankets. He had forgotten to turn off the overhead light, and the curtains were wide open. On one elbow, leaning over her, he studied her face.

In the clear light of day, her skin was luminous. The blue of her eyes was darker today, perhaps reflecting the navy comforter. She looked at him as she always did, wary, on her guard. As if expecting at any moment to have him lash out at her.

Couldn't she feel how much he needed her…needed this? He'd taken her like a wild man, over and over again this weekend. And as soon as they finished one round, he wanted her again.

Lightly, he mapped her body with his fingertips. She was slender, but not skinny. No ribs protruding, no hollowed-out collarbone. Everything about her was the epitome of life and health. When he cupped her breast, she turned her head away.

He took her chin and made her look at him. "What are you afraid I'll see in your eyes?" he asked quietly.

"Nothing," she said. Long lashes at half-mast cloaked her secrets.

"Tell me, Annalise," he said gently. "We're the ones writing the rules here. I won't make fun of anything you say, I swear."

She moved restlessly, dislodging his hand and sitting up with the sheet pulled to her armpits. Grief darkened her eyes even further as she finally stared straight at him. "You know too much about me," she said, her voice ragged.

"And it scares me that when we're together…sexually…I feel exposed."

"Surely you've been intimate with a number of men."

"Not as many as you think. And besides…"

This time he waited in silence, not prompting her. The honest, unvarnished truth was something he had wanted badly. Now that she was giving it, he had to struggle to sort out his feelings.

Annalise lifted her chin. "I am not an easy woman, Sam. I know that. I have baggage. Both in general, and where you are concerned."

He shrugged. "All of us have baggage."

She frowned. "I don't want to get close to you."

He absorbed the shot, felt it pierce his heart. "I see."

"I don't think you do. Maybe it's just the difference between men and women, or maybe it's my own neuroses. But when we're naked…intimate…it feels as if you take more than I want to give."

"I'm not your enemy," he said, his fists clenched beneath the blanket where she couldn't see. He'd forced himself to remain in a seemingly relaxed position, reclining on his side. But the pretense was wearing thin.

"You're not my anything. That's the problem. We've succumbed to the urge to scratch an itch, probably because we're snowed in and we're both reasonably attractive people, but that's as far as it goes."

He felt the ground shift beneath his feet. "What if it could be more?"

Something flickered in her eyes, a lightning flash of deep emotion that was gone before he could analyze it. He hadn't meant to say the words. They had surprised him as much as her.

"What do you mean?" She was prevaricating…buying time.

"What if we started over? No expectations. A future wide open. Maybe we've both been wrong about what we want. Are you willing to take a chance that we've been too blind to see the truth?"

For a few shimmering seconds, a door into her soul opened. He recognized it without question. He'd stake his life on it. In her eyes he saw the hope and the fear. The dawning realization that things could be different. He was pretty sure he even saw a laughing baby with her eyes and his chin.

He didn't want to push. Not with the chance that she might actually come to him on her own. But he was so damn close to something momentous, it made him ache. "Talk to me, honey," he urged. "Please."

He shouldn't have asked. She wasn't ready. And when she did what he begged of her, the truth hurt more than he could have thought possible.

"You're not making sense, Sam," she said flatly. "I've never known a man more sure of himself, and I told you from the beginning that the weekend was all I was offering."

"God, you're impossible," he shouted. It took a lot, as a rule, for him to lose his temper, but with Annalise, the fuse stayed lit half the time. "How can you be such a coward?"

She went white, and at that exact instant, the front doorbell rang, echoing far away in the house.

Her eyes widened as Sam cursed. "I'll get rid of whoever it is."

He went to the window and peeked out, groaning in disbelief when he read the side of the truck parked in the driveway.

Annalise had scrambled onto her knees. "What is it? What's wrong?"

Sam reached in his suitcase and grabbed a clean pair

of pants and a long-sleeve knit shirt. "Unless I'm mistaken, it's the guy who's going to overhaul the heat and air system."

"But they're not supposed to arrive until tomorrow. How did they get here?"

"A lot of the snow has melted, and they have a heavy gauge vehicle with good tires. What can I say, Annalise? I guess you can consider this your version of saved by the bell. Unless there's something you want to say to me. Right now. Do you, darlin'? Am I really so scary?"

Again that glimpse, that sliver of heaven shining in the darkness. Her lips parted as she started to speak…he felt something tighten in his chest.

But the noise below shattered any last hope of taking a step forward.

Annalise shook her head slowly. "I think we've said it all, Sam. I'm sorry."

He left the room so quickly, she was stunned. Since pajamas were her only option on this floor, she scuttled downstairs wrapped in a sheet and disappeared into her room. By the time she came out fifteen minutes later, fully dressed, Sam was entertaining in the living room. "What have I missed?" she asked, summoning a smile as she assessed the situation.

Sam gave her a chilly smile that perhaps only she realized had an edge to it. "This is Darren Harrell and his wife, Rachel. The little boy is their son, Butch."

Rachel cuddled an infant, her expression anxious. "I'm sorry if we've intruded. Darren called Mrs. Ely and she said it was okay for us to come a day early and to bring the baby. We live in a really rural area, and the heavy wet snow took down all kinds of power lines. If it was just us, we could get by, but I couldn't let the baby stay there. And we only have one vehicle right now."

Annalise took the woman's free hand and squeezed it. "Don't be silly. I'm here to work, as well. And you're not intruding…right, Sam?"

He leaned in the doorway, his smile genuine as he aimed it at the visitors. "Of course not. This old house has tons of bedrooms. I'll help bring in your things. Annalise, do you mind getting them set up in whichever room you ladies decide is best?"

"With pleasure."

While the men were outside, Annalise gave Rachel an abbreviated tour. "How about this bedroom?" she asked, throwing open the door. "It's fairly large and has its own bathroom. The painting hasn't been done yet, and it's missing some finishing touches, but it's serviceable."

Rachel smiled shyly, the baby propped on her hip. "We'll be fine." Though the younger woman was dressed in worn denims and an inexpensive sweatshirt, she had a sunny disposition that proclaimed louder than words that she was happy with her lot in life. While Annalise watched, Rachel put the infant on the bed and efficiently changed a wet diaper. "Butch is such a good baby…he hardly ever cries. You won't even know he's here."

Annalise chuckled. "I'm not worried."

Suddenly, Rachel exclaimed, "Oh, gosh. I promised my mom I'd let her know when we got here. She's a worrier, and the snow was an issue. Hold Butch for me, will you?"

Before Annalise had a chance to protest, Rachel thrust the infant into her arms and disappeared. The sudden change in circumstances put a lump in Annalise's throat. She couldn't remember the last time she'd held a small child. As a rule, she avoided them whenever possible.

Her hands shaky, she held the kid at arm's length and stared at him. "Well, you drew the short straw, kiddo. I'm clueless. Are we supposed to play peek-a-boo? Or maybe I burp you? Do you just hang out when you're not hungry?"

Butch had wild red hair and gorgeous blue eyes. After gazing at her solemnly for several seconds, he smiled, cooing and blowing bubbles that collected on his chubby chin. A single tooth at the bottom of his mouth shone proudly.

Her heart contracted in her chest and her womb quivered. This was why she stayed far away from adorable little rug rats. They made her ache for what she was afraid she could never have. She touched her nose to the baby's, talking silly nonsense syllables to him. When he chortled, she pulled him close, nuzzling his cheek and patting his back as he rooted at her shoulder.

Her blouse was silk, a new offering from an up-and-coming Parisian designer. It never occurred to her that she should keep him away from her expensive outfit. Instead, she held him close, inhaling the precious smells of baby powder and shampoo and a scent unique to small human beings.

She kissed the top of his head. "That's okay, little fella. You and I will do just fine. I promise not to drop you and you try not to poop before your mama gets back."

Eleven

Sam stood stock-still, suitcases in hand, and felt his heart fall somewhere down around his feet. The smile Annalise aimed at Butch—the fabulous, cajoling, entirely unguarded beam of happiness—was one Sam had never witnessed. The look on her face as she bounced her little charge was heartbreaking in its rarity.

Why had Sam never seen her like this? Open, delighted, intensely feminine in her gentle care of another woman's child.

"He likes you," Sam said, setting the luggage just inside the door and lingering there.

Annalise whirled to face him, her cheeks pink. "Isn't he cute?"

Butch was wearing John Deere overalls and a yellow onesie with long sleeves. On his tiny feet were soft cloth tennis shoes that matched his outfit.

Sam grinned, enjoying the show. "He could use a barber, but yeah, he's a peach."

Annalise held him out. "You want to take a turn?"

It hit him in that moment that she had been hiding herself from him the entire weekend. Never once had he seen this side of her, the soft, nurturing affection, the unselfconscious pleasure.

The knowledge grieved him, for it spelled doom to any fledgling dreams he might have been weaving. Annalise didn't want to be in a relationship with him. She didn't want intimacy, roots, commitment. She was afraid of what he made her feel. Of what they both felt. Because she didn't trust the feelings and she didn't trust Sam. Seeing her now, with a baby, made him face the unspoken yearnings that had sprung up deep in his gut.

He tasted the bitter bile of failure and found it to be more painful to swallow than he could have imagined. Watching Annalise hold a small child reminded him of everything he didn't yet have in his life. And it also pointed out that a woman who could show two such different faces to him was someone with issues.

He had his own demons to fight…the specter of statistical marital failure, the possibility that he might be no better a father than his own dad had been. But at least he knew in those instances what battles he faced. When it came to Annalise, there were depths he'd been unable to reach in her, secrets she wouldn't share. And the fact that he had only now realized he was perilously close to falling ass over heels in love with her didn't help in the least.

He shook his head, backing out into the hall, feeling appalled and clumsy and off balance. "You keep him. Darren needs my help."

When he went back outside, he found Rachel wrapping up a phone call. Sam lowered his voice. "The kitchen is stocked. But Annalise doesn't cook and she's self-conscious about it. Feel free to take over the meal planning for as long as you're here."

Rachel nodded. "It's the least I can do."

Over dinner, the conversation between four very different adults was helped along by little Butch's antics. His parents had brought every conceivable baby conveyance, including a high chair. Rachel had matter-of-factly prepared country ham and hash brown potatoes for dinner, along with a simple serving of applesauce.

Annalise was subdued, but held her own in the odd social setting. Sam had no appetite at all, because all he could think about was that he had missed his last chance this afternoon. He couldn't stay any longer. He wouldn't. It was too painful.

As soon as it was polite, he stood and carried his plate to the sink. "Thanks for the dinner. I'm going to head back to Charlottesville. Tomorrow will be a full day."

When he turned around, Annalise's face was the color of milk. "You're leaving now?"

He nodded tersely. "I have a business to run, and now that Darren and Rachel are here to keep you company, there's no reason for me to stay."

"But what about the snow and your car?"

"I checked the forecast. The temperature is still above freezing…and will stay that way. I'll follow the truck tracks Darren made until I get back out to the highway. He said all the main roads have been plowed and salted."

"But…" Her eyes shimmered with anguish.

Seeing her reaction almost made his resolution buckle. Perhaps if he stayed, they could continue their aborted conversation. "But what, Annalise? Can you think of a reason I should hang around?" Their guests had disappeared seconds before to the back of the house to change a poopy diaper.

She stood and faced him, her arms wrapped around her waist. "You're angry with me." .

He shrugged. "Maybe."

"For what?"

His jaw worked as he filtered through the words that wanted to tumble forth uncensored. "You told me that this weekend was as far as you were willing to go. Have you changed your mind?"

Annalise was no fool. She heard the question behind the question. *Are you willing to take a chance and see where we end up?*

With every cell and sinew in his body he willed her to say yes, to come to him with a smile and hug and tell him she wanted him to stay. But she didn't.

At that moment, the Harrells returned. Darren held Butch as Rachel started cleaning up. With a baseball cap on backward and a scraggly mustache that was almost too blond to be noticeable, the skinny young contractor barely looked old enough to be a dad.

He held Butch easily, tucked in his left arm like a football. "I hate to inconvenience you, Miss Annalise, but you'll probably need to leave here Wednesday morning. By that time I'll be done with the preliminary stuff, and my crew will arrive to start ripping out the old duct work."

"What about Rachel and the baby?" Sam asked.

"My mom's coming from Roanoke to pick them up that morning. She and my dad have been asking for a long visit with Butch, and this seemed like the perfect time. Me and the boys will have sleeping bags and a few electric heaters, 'cause the furnace won't be online at all until Friday night or Saturday morning. Maybe Monday if we run into any hitches. After that y'all can come and go as you please, warm as toast."

Annalise nodded. "That makes sense. But you'll have to sign for any shipments that arrive before I get back. I've started ordering a lot of the paint and wallpaper and draperies."

"No problem. And you don't have to worry. My guys will leave everything as nice as when they found it. We'll camp out in the living room…won't even need to mess up the bedrooms."

Sam frowned. "That's not necessary. I know my grandmother would expect you to make yourselves at home. Especially since commuting each day isn't a viable option."

Rachel wiped her hands on a dish towel, grinning. "Don't worry, Mr. Ely. He's been looking forward to this for days."

The younger couple left, ready to get settled in their room and put the baby down for the night.

Sam exhaled slowly. "I'm going to head upstairs and pack. If it's not too much trouble, why don't you put all our wet snow clothes in the dryer."

He brought up the subject on purpose, curious to see how she would react.

Annalise nodded, not meeting his eyes. "Of course."

Drawing this out was futile. He ground his teeth together, fighting almost irresistible temptation. "Goodbye, Princess. I'll see you around."

Feeling like an old man, he turned to leave.

"Wait," she said urgently, her voice breathless. "Won't you at least come tell me goodbye before you go?"

He turned back, though he knew he shouldn't. She stood there tall and poised and yet with a hint of melancholy. "If you want me to."

"I do."

Upstairs in his bedroom, he threw things haphazardly into his large bag. He didn't want to go into the bathroom, couldn't bear to look at the shower and remember. He grabbed his toiletries, stopping dead when he saw his face in the mirror. Where had those lines on his forehead come from? Or the evidence of stress in his posture and on his jaw? He looked as if he were at the end of his rope.

Cursing roughly, he returned to the bedroom, gave one last sweeping glance at the bureau and then stopped dead. Piled on a straight-back chair in the corner were Annalise's pretty feminine pajamas. He picked up the top and held it to his face, his eyes stinging. God, he was a fool.

For seven years…seven long, damn years. Beautiful, sexy Annalise Wolff had tormented him with her icy silences and her cool, accusing gaze. Now…finally, she had given him a taste of what it could be like between them. She had connected with Sam in a way he'd only dreamed about. They were damned near perfect in bed together.

In two short days, he had second-guessed everything he thought he knew about his goals for the future, had even tried to convince himself that he and Annalise might have what it took to be a couple, in spite of their differences. But she wasn't going to let it happen. And he didn't know why.

The reason didn't really matter. He dropped the soft cloth as if it had burned his hand, and scrubbed both palms over his face. He was finished. It was over.

He loaded the car and sat in the front seat to call his grandparents and update them on what was going on. His grandmother asked a few seemingly innocent questions, and Sam had to wonder, at least for a moment, if she had hired Annalise with some kind of matchmaking in mind.

When he hung up, he looked at the house, warm light gleaming through Gram's lace curtains. Some of the happiest times of his life had been spent in that house, this weekend included. Would he ever be able to bring a wife and family here without encountering the memory of Annalise's sex-rumpled hair and sparkling eyes?

He rubbed his chest, feeling an ache that wouldn't go away. If he could understand where he'd screwed up, he'd be able to fix things. Surely Annalise wasn't still holding on to the past. No way could she doubt the sincerity of his apology or the intensity of his attraction to her. They'd damn near burned up the sheets.

But it hit him then that perhaps he didn't know her at all. Maybe she enjoyed luring men into her web and destroying them. The black-widow analogy disturbed him. She wasn't cold or calculating. The worst he could say about her was that she was insecure.

The sheer absurdity of that thought forced a laugh. He was probably the only person on the planet who would describe her that way. The woman was hell on wheels, kicking ass and taking names on a daily basis. She was full of life and sass and enthusiasm.

Except where Sam was concerned. Around him, she acted like she wanted him and hated herself for doing so. Maybe that was harsh. At times he had felt a softening in her, a simple pleasure in the heat they generated together. He felt as if they had lived a lifetime in the last forty-eight hours, the past and the present coming together in a cataclysm of epic proportion.

Drumming his fingers on the steering wheel, he debated taking the easy way out and simply driving away. But as Annalise had so helpfully pointed out on a number of occasions, the world expected Sam Ely to do the honorable thing.

He'd told Annalise he would say goodbye. No way around it.

She was standing in the foyer when he opened the front door. "I thought you'd left," she said, her voice subdued.

The wind caught the door, jerking it out of his hand and slamming it. "Sorry," he said. "I told you I would say goodbye. I'm not a liar."

"You could have forgotten. You have a lot on your mind."

He shoved his hands in his pockets to keep from grabbing her. "I'll tell Gram you have everything under control."

"I'll send you email updates with photos. You can forward them to her."

So polite, so bloody polite. He hadn't planned to ask, but the question wouldn't be ignored any longer. "Have you forgiven me for what happened when you were twenty-one?"

She shrugged. "Of course."

"No *of course* about it. We've barely spoken in seven years."

"True."

"Is that what we're going back to?" he asked bluntly. "Veiled hostility?"

"I doubt I'll have much occasion to speak to you when you're with your wife and kids."

The sentence held equal measures of sarcasm and stoicism. He searched her face. What the hell did she want from him? "In that case," he said, feeling the dual punches of anger and need, "I'd better take what I can get right now."

Perhaps he grabbed her or maybe she launched herself at him, but whichever way it happened, she whispered his name as they ended up desperate in each other's arms. She kissed him as wildly as he kissed her. Tongues thrust and mated, breathing harshened.

Beneath her thin blouse her nipples were hard pebbles. His sex was equally firm, pushing urgently at her belly.

"Do you want me to stay?" he asked, giving her one more chance to claim what was hers. It didn't matter that she was nothing like the image of a woman he'd always imagined building a life with. He *wanted* her…not in spite of the difference, but because of it. She was perfect for him.

She laid her head against his collarbone, squeezed her arms around his waist and then released him, outwardly calm but for the rise and fall of her chest. "I don't need you to stay," she said. "With Rachel and Darren here, I'll be fine."

She hadn't answered his question. She'd talked about *need,* not want. "God, you're stubborn." He said it quietly, no accusation in his words. Only sadness. "See you around, Princess."

When he walked out the door and closed it behind him, he could see her silhouette…tall, slim, alone.

Annalise didn't know it was possible to have your heart ripped from your chest and still function as a living, breathing human. For two hours, she sat with the Harrells in the living room, playing Monopoly, talking about current events, speculating about the economy. She couldn't bear to go to her room and see the bed where Sam had made love to her.

The baby woke up around nine. Rachel fetched him, his little face blotchy from crying. "Poor thing is teething," she said, "and this is a strange house to him. But it's okay, isn't it, darlin'?" She smooched the top of his head and held him to her breast.

Before he left, Sam had brought down a rocking chair from his grandparents' bedroom. Annalise looked at the infant with barely concealed longing. "May I rock him for a bit? Do you mind?"

Rachel and Darren laughed in unison. Rachel tucked a thin blanket around Butch's legs and handed him over. "Believe me, hon, we'll take all the help we can get."

For a while, silence reigned in the room. Again, a warm fire crackled. Rachel found a pencil and a book of sudoku. Darren brought in a beautiful guitar from his truck and began to sing old ballads.

Annalise rocked slowly, immersing herself in the exquisite, bone-deep peace of holding the tiny body that very quickly went limp against her shoulder. She looked over Butch's head at his parents. "How do you know what to do?" she asked.

Rachel looked up, nibbling the end of the pencil. "What do you mean?"

"How did you learn to be a mother?"

"Oh, Lord, honey. It's called trial and error. No two babies are alike. We got lucky on this one, but my best friend has a kid with colic. They haven't slept in six months. There's no manual. I call my mother if I really get spooked. And Darren, here, is a rock in the middle of the night when we're both at our wit's end. But it all comes down to loving Butch. We do *what* we have to *when* we have to. That's all there is to parenting. It's no secret formula."

Annalise nodded, not that she really understood. It had to be more complicated than that. Otherwise, there wouldn't be so many awful parents.

Rachel, for all her youth, and she couldn't be much more than nineteen, seemed mature beyond her years. She eyed Annalise gravely. "Haven't you ever been around any babies, Miss Annalise?"

"No. Not really. I was the youngest in my family."

"Are you one of the Wolffs? Darren said he thought he recognized you from your pictures in the paper."

Oh, hell. Make that *crap*. She couldn't even give up cussing in her own head. And no matter what she did, she could never escape the notoriety of being a Wolff. "I am. The only girl in the bunch." She said it lightly, but she wondered what Rachel was thinking.

"It must have been hard…growing up around all that testosterone."

Annalise grimaced. "You could say that. They couldn't decide whether to coddle me or to toughen me up."

Darren stopped playing momentarily, curiosity written on his raw-boned face. "Which won out?"

Annalise thought about it for a moment. She'd never really analyzed how her family treated her, but oddly enough, it dawned on her that it was a mixture of both. "Depends on the day," she whispered, not wanting to wake the baby. "They act like I'm one of them when it comes to sports or arguing politics. But when we hit on the subject of my adult life and my ability to run it as I see fit, we sometimes break ranks."

Rachel nodded slowly. "They want to wrap you in cotton. I know the feeling. There are three of us girls, and my daddy thinks we're still ten years old and wearing pigtails."

Darren lit into a lullaby, his rough tenor slightly off-key, but pleasing nevertheless. "If I ever have a girl," he said, pausing as the guitar wandered through the chorus, "it will be the same. Daddies and their daughters have something special."

Annalise and Rachel laughed, ruefully acknowledging a universal truth.

Rachel stood and reached for the baby. "He'll go down for the night now. I'd better turn in, too. The little rascal will be up at dawn."

As Annalise watched, Darren tucked his guitar away and went to put his arm around his wife and son. "Thanks for the hospitality, ma'am. I know Rachel will be glad of the company."

"Me, too," Annalise said. "Me, too."

She went through the house, extinguishing all the lights. Everywhere she looked, she saw Sam. Laughing, frowning, teasing, seducing. He'd filled the house with his charm and his personality, and now, even with the advent of three visitors, the rooms felt empty and forlorn.

Her bedroom was even worse. The second time he'd made love to her was right here…on this mattress, face-to-face. Now, with Sam long gone, it was hard to believe it had happened. Maybe this weekend was all a dream.

She'd fantasized plenty about Sam Ely over the years. And wondered, if she hadn't thrown herself at him so blatantly, whether she might have had a chance later…when she was older.

Well, she was older now. And Sam…wow. Sam was in his prime. And still unattached. As she climbed into bed, she thought about all the women she had seen him date over the years. Each relationship, no matter how long or short, had broken her heart. And when each one ended, a tiny flicker of hope had valiantly remained lit in her heart.

She had believed, with incredible naïveté, that as long as Sam was still on the market, there was a chance.

Now, thanks to her job, she had stumbled upon her opportunity. She'd been locked up, all alone with Sam for forty-eight hours, give or take a few. And the sparks had flown. So much so, that she felt singed by the fire. She and Sam were sexually compatible, that much was clear. A man couldn't fake pleasure to that extent. Sam wanted her.

But wanting wasn't enough.

Though he had begged her to give them a chance—with

every seeming evidence of sincerity—his words had to be weighed in the context of forced proximity, sexual excess and the cold light of day. Annalise wanted to say yes...so much that it hurt her chest to hold back. But she had to be strong enough for both of them. Strong enough to say no.

Sam deserved to have his perfect woman. He was too good a man to settle for less than that. And she cared about him too much to begin something that would disappoint him in the end.

After finally falling into a fitful sleep, she awakened abruptly sometime around 3:00 a.m. Her heart pounding, she listened for whatever sound had disturbed her. Unfortunately, this time she wasn't going to find Sam huddled in front of the fire trying to get warm.

Pulling on her robe and slippers, she stepped into the hall and saw light coming from beneath the living room door. A baby's cry disturbed the silence of the sleeping house.

Rachel looked up when Annalise entered the room. "I'm so sorry," she said. "I was trying to calm him in our bedroom. But Darren has so much work to do tomorrow, and he needs his rest."

Annalise pulled an ottoman close to the rocking chair and sat down. "Don't be silly. I sometimes prowl around the house at night. Most women I know are light sleepers."

"I've always thought that was God's way of making us ready for motherhood."

That one simple statement struck Annalise with the force of a lightning bolt. Could it be that easy? Were women born with an inherent capability for nurturing? She reached for hazy memories of her mother, trying to catch a vision of bedtime songs, snuggly hugs, storybooks read together. Nothing came to mind except an uneasy feeling in the pit of her stomach.

"Why don't you let me tend to him for the rest of the night? You must be exhausted. If you trust me, that is," she said hurriedly. "Don't feel like you have to. I know I'm a stranger."

Rachel closed her eyes and sighed. "I shouldn't say yes. Butch is my baby, not yours. But Lord knows, the thought of a few uninterrupted hours of sleep sounds like heaven right now."

"Then do it. I swear I'll guard him with my life, and if he's inconsolable, I'll come get you."

"You talked me into it. Let me go change him, and I'll bring the diaper bag back with me."

As mom and baby departed, Annalise added logs to the simmering coals in the fireplace, and soon a cheery blaze roared. She dragged the generous-sized sofa in front of the hearth, her cheeks heating as she thought of what she and Sam had done on this very piece of furniture. It was humbling to realize that he lived in her thoughts constantly. Even though he had physically left the premises, the memories remained, tantalizing and vivid.

Butch was still fussing when Rachel returned. She handed Annalise a teether. "Let him suck on the hard side. It might help." She paused, her nose crinkling. "Are you sure about this? It might be a long night."

"Don't worry about me," Annalise said, taking Butch from her arms. "Consider it a show of support from one woman to another. We females have to stick together."

Rachel's grin was tired. "I'll owe you one."

When she left, Annalise stared down at Butch. His eyes were puffy from crying. His nose was snotty, and his cheeks were cherry-red. "Poor darlin'. We'll get by. You'll see."

She sat down in the rocker, trying to get him to latch on to the teether, but he was having none of that. At last, she cradled him on her breast, stroking his downy-soft head as he snuffled and squirmed. At least he wasn't full-out bawling. That might have rattled a novice like Annalise. But this she could handle.

When he simply wouldn't be still, even with the rocker moving to and fro in a steady motion, Annalise began to sing. An old Billy Joel ballad her father liked, a Sheryl Crow song about soaking up the sun, several Adele numbers. At last little Butch sighed deeply and began to relax.

Annalise's own eyes were heavy. She wondered why she had always been so scared of this. Rachel was right. Much of it was instinctive. Of course, that was easy to say with the child's parents just down the hall. It might be a whole different story if she held her own fussy baby.

But then again, with the right man for help and support, how bad could it be?

Idly patting the little boy's back, she felt the smooth nap of his pajamas. Soft, so soft. And Sam wanted three or four of these. A family, a bulwark against the world, a unit bound by love and belonging.

Soon, Gracie and Gareth's baby would arrive. Annalise had a feeling that other little ones wouldn't be far behind. Wolff Mountain would once again echo with childish laughter.

Her hands trembled as a wave of longing swept through her, leaving her spent and weak. She had sent Sam away. Because she was afraid of failing. Failing as a woman. Sam's kind of woman. Motherhood didn't offer do-overs. And Sam wanted babies. Plural.

But what if she were wrong? What if her unconventional past was no longer relevant? Sam seemed to like her the way she was. Were her insecurities about her femininity nothing more than habit? What if Annalise Wolff had a maternal instinct despite all odds? And not just that...what if she had the ability to be the kind of woman Sam needed, the kind of woman who trusted in herself, believed in herself and opened her heart to share love?

Butch was sound asleep now, his tiny snore a miracle in itself. Carefully, she stood, moving toward the sofa. Laying him down for a brief instant, she stoked the fire and replaced the screen. Grabbing the pile of covers she had gathered earlier, she eased down oh-so-carefully, positioning her body with her back to the fire and Butch tucked carefully between her and the back cushion.

Their little nest was surprisingly comfortable. She wanted to savor the experience, to file it away to pull out and remember on another day. But her eyes were heavy, and she succumbed to sleep.

Twelve

Sam wasn't worth a damn when he got back from the country. It was business as usual in his office Monday morning, and for the first time in years he didn't care about any of it. The interns were patently disappointed to see him. They had been looking forward to their sanctioned reign. Too bad the weather hadn't cooperated and kept Sam stranded.

The late January warm-up and a dose of undiluted sunshine appeared to be making everyone happy and cheerful. Everyone but Sam. A man known for his easygoing disposition, he shocked himself and most of his staff by snapping and growling. At last he resorted to hiding out in his inner office to keep from doing bodily harm to anyone who dared cross him.

He ached with missing Annalise. Memories of their lovemaking taunted him, keeping him hard and frustrated. The days and nights he'd spent with her seemed like a dream…except for the fact that he could still smell her perfume on his clothes.

Like a lovesick schoolboy, he'd kept those flannel shirts out of the laundry hamper, unable to erase her presence from his life. She was difficult and challenging and sexy as hell. More than any woman he had ever known, Annalise Wolff satisfied the hunger in him, a need that was as much emotional as physical.

The only thing keeping him sane was the knowledge that on Wednesday morning she would be coming back to the city, and he'd at least be able to see her at the office. Thank God for Darren and his crew.

From the moment Sam drove away from the farm, his brain had wrestled with a problem that had no answer. For years he'd been trying to find the perfect woman, the one who would give him his perfect family. And now, in one of fate's perverse games of chance, he'd fallen in love with the one woman who not only didn't trust him, but who also was the antithesis of everything he thought he wanted.

He could move on…keep looking for a suitable candidate. The trouble was, he was pretty sure he couldn't live without Annalise Wolff. Which meant he had some big decisions to make. He'd give her until Wednesday evening to miss him, and then he was going to claim what was his.

Annalise loved him. He had to believe that. Because the alternative was simply unacceptable.

Annalise loved having the Harrells underfoot. The house buzzed with noise and laughter, Darren measured and crawled into the basement and ordered parts. Rachel cooked and entertained the baby, and was well on the way to being a new, honest-to-goodness friend. Annalise felt comfortable around her. And despite their differences in lifestyle and finances, Rachel was not intimidated by Annalise.

Monday, before dinner, something odd struck Annalise. So much so that she marched into the kitchen and asked, "It only now occurred to me that you took over the meal preparation duties when you arrived. Not that I mind… I've loved it, but how did that happen? You don't strike me as the kind of woman who would waltz in and take over someone else's kitchen."

Butch was tucked into a high chair gobbling Cheerios. Rachel's face turned pink. "Well, um…"

"Spill it, woman, I won't bite."

Rachel shrugged. "Mr. Ely pulled me aside and asked me, soon after we arrived. He said you couldn't cook and that you were self-conscious about it. He didn't want you to feel uncomfortable."

"I see." Annalise digested that, feeling a little fillip of warmth in her chest. Sam really was a gentleman. But it seemed thoughtfulness was simply his default setting. It didn't mean he cared about Annalise. "Well, he's right. About the not cooking, I mean. Carry on with my blessing and my gratitude."

"Do you not like to cook?" Rachel asked, her gentle smile curious.

"It's a long story. And pretty boring. Let's just chalk it up to growing up with in an all-male household."

"I get it. The culinary arts weren't high on the list."

"More like repairing foreign cars and learning to fly a helicopter."

Rachel's eyes rounded. "You can really do that?"

"Yeah. If someone put a gun to my head. My father and uncle use one for both business and pleasure. I stopped riding in it a long time ago…and have lobbied fiercely for them to get rid of it. But no one listens to me."

"Wow. You're really something, Annalise. I'm glad we got to know each other."

The compliment was heartfelt, sincere. Annalise accepted it as such, realizing with a sort of dazed puzzlement that perhaps other people were not as dismissive of her accomplishments as she was.

Clearing her throat of some emotion that constricted her words, she said, "Thank you. You're pretty amazing, as well."

By the time Wednesday morning arrived, Annalise had a good grasp of which rooms would require the most work and which furniture needed to be donated, pending Mrs. Ely's approval. The weather was fabulous, and though the ground was muddy in the wake of the snowmelt, it felt good to be outside.

After breakfast, in preparation for leaving, she wandered the perimeter of the house, trying to imagine Sam and his mythical family staying there. Already she hated the woman in the picture. Annalise wanted to be her.

She stopped dead, her toes curling in her borrowed rubber boots as the truth hit her. *Holy hell. She wanted to have Sam's babies. All of them...however many the good Lord chose to send their way.*

Swaying on her feet, she told herself to snap out of it. Sam didn't want her. Well, that wasn't exactly true. He enjoyed her body. *He enjoyed her body.* That's all it was. Sex. Plain and simple.

Only, with Sam, sex was the furthest thing from simple. It was world-altering, unprecedented. In his arms, she felt complete, she felt feminine, desired. And that feeling of fulfillment allowed her for the first time in her life to see another choice, another way.

Sam had opened the door to possibilities. Had practically begged her to take a chance, to be the daring, adventuresome woman the world thought she was. Sprawled in his bed after their last, erotic shower, he had laid his cards on the table. *Are you willing to take a chance that we've been too blind to see the truth?* Sam had been brave enough to take the first step, to initiate a shift toward something far more profound even than physical pleasure.

But she had fallen into old habits of self-protection. And in doing so, had sent him away. Afraid to be hurt again, terrified of the idea of bringing children into the world. Scared that Sam would look at her with disappointment and regret. She deserved the pain that made her chest ache with grief too deep for tears.

She might have been brought up in a household of men, true. And yes, she had many skills not typically regarded as "womanly." But Sam liked her the way she was. He'd said so on more than one occasion. And surprisingly, he'd taught her to see herself as he did…and to accept and appreciate what she saw.

A man like that was rare and wonderful. So it was about time she got her act together and went after him.

A couple of hours later, she stopped at a Walmart in a suburb outside of Charlottesville. It was a safe choice, with little likelihood that she would run into anyone she knew. Jittery and anxious, she knew she wouldn't be able to tolerate small talk. Plus, she didn't want to have to explain what she was doing.

Grabbing a shopping cart, feeling more than a little self-conscious, she headed for the housewares department and began throwing things in the basket. Twenty-five minutes later, she scoured the grocery aisles. All in all, "Project Sam" took just under an hour.

She shook her head in self-derision as she headed back

out to her car. Grand gestures were more expensive than she realized. It was a good thing she had money to burn. Which reminded her, she needed to send Rachel and Darren a really nice baby gift, even if it was a bit belated.

When she arrived in Charlottesville, her condo welcomed her with stale air and half-dead plants. She'd forgotten to water them…again. For a moment, the old insecurity surfaced. How could she take care of a baby? She'd been reared by a bad mother for a brief period of her life, and then no mother at all. Her formative years had been influenced by air rifles, fist fights and playing army ambush in the forest surrounding Wolff Castle.

Her brain whirled while, on autopilot, she put away the cold groceries and unloaded her luggage from the car. After her fourth trip, she shook her head in disgust. Maybe Sam was right. Maybe she *was* high-maintenance. It had never been a problem. Her father had indulged her every wish. But in any situation when a baby came into the picture, everything had to change.

She didn't want to think of herself as a selfish person. Charity, both via her checkbook and her volunteer hours, was important to her. And she cared deeply about her family. But being a mother was so much more. It involved self-sacrifice and a consistent determination to put another person's needs first.

Could she be that woman for Sam? For herself? For a newborn?

She sat down hard, clutching a bag of flour. Terror and exhilaration squeezed her chest in equal measures. Suddenly, the future taunted her with bright possibilities. But she was not so naive as to ignore the flip side of the coin. If she tried to change and failed, the consequences were unthinkable.

* * *

Sam left work Wednesday night before 6:00 p.m. His relatively prompt homecoming was such an anomaly, he knew he was in trouble. All day, he had imagined Annalise in her car, driving the interstate, heading back to him.

His hand shook as he put a key in the lock of his loft-turned-condo. All he wanted during the next half hour was a shower, a change of clothes and a few quiet minutes to decide if the plan he was contemplating was total suicide.

As soon as he opened the door, he groaned inwardly, cursing life's capricious sense of humor. His mother was in residence, God help him.

"Hi, sweet pea," she said, enveloping him in a cloud of Obsession, a tight hug and a Southern accent so thick it took him back in time for an instant.

"Mom," he said, grimacing inwardly and fiercely regretting that he had ever given her a key. "What are you doing here?" He loved her dearly, but after he'd hit his mid-thirties, she'd been at DEFCON 1 in her campaign to marry him off. Her pop-in visits, often with some co-conspirator in tow, were usually poorly disguised match-making attempts.

Charlaine Ely smiled broadly, clad in a stylish winter suit that belied her age. "Can't a momma visit her baby? Come in the kitchen and see Daphne. You're gonna love what she's fixin' for us."

Annalise had broken her New Year's Eve resolution so many times and in so many ways, she probably should have her mouth washed out with soap. Cooking was damned hard. The FCC needed to take a bunch of those Cooking Channel chefs to court for false advertising.

At long last, her creation was finished. She stared at the cake on her trashed kitchen counter with misgivings.

Although it was supposed to be round and two-layered, it had ended up more of a free-form shape with a distinct dip in the middle. Disguising it the best she could with icing, she finally gave up and decided it was the thought that counted. The cake was resting on a cardboard circle she'd bought when she got the groceries. Hell, she didn't even own any Tupperware. She'd had to buy a knockoff.

Getting the cake into the carrier was a bit like forcing a beloved pet into a cage for a trip to the vet. The cake didn't want to go. In the end, she had to use her bare hands, which unfortunately meant ripping off part of the icing in the process, and thus having to make another half batch to cover up her boo-boos.

She decided to clean up the kitchen when she got back. Nobody was going to be around to see the disaster anyway. Her outfit was ruined, so she dashed into the bedroom and grabbed a pair of designer jeans and a winter-white cashmere turtleneck. One dash of eyeliner, a fillip of mascara and a swish of lip gloss, and she was ready. High-maintenance indeed.

The trip to Sam's condo was less than ten miles, but the drive felt like it took an eternity. She hadn't exactly worked out what she was going to say when she saw him. She was hoping that her peace offering and perhaps some quick and kinky sex might ease the way.

Tapping her fingers on the steering wheel as she idled at a red light, her thighs quivered and her breasts grew heavy and tight as she contemplated his welcome. *Please, God, don't let him be mad.*

He was well within his rights to be furious. The last time they'd been together, he'd asked *her* to ask *him* to stay. But instead of meeting his overture halfway, she had practically shoved him out the door in a futile effort to prove to herself that she didn't need Sam.

What an idiot she was.

Thank God she had come to her senses. But what if it was too late? The prospect of seeing condemnation in his eyes—disgust, even—shriveled her soul. Sam's opinion mattered to her. It always had. Which was why she was prepared to grovel today if necessary. She had a big speech to make and she wanted desperately for it to go well. Maybe Sam would be in a forgiving mood.

Ruefully, she realized that the last time she had been this nervous was the evening she propositioned Sam when she was twenty-one. That day had ended in disaster. Though her stomach clenched and twisted, she refused to dwell on the negative. Sam cared about her. And this time, she knew beyond the shadow of a doubt that he wanted her sexually.

Relationships were founded on far less all the time. But she had really screwed up with Sam.

Was he going to believe the truth? That she had changed her entire world view on the basis of one magical weekend? That she was willing to consider the possibility of a grown-up relationship…of children?

She found a parking spot on the street, got out on shaky legs and locked the car with a flip of the button on the door. Unfortunately, her keys were on the seat beside the cake box.

Damn, damn, damn…

She would *not* cry. Tears were girly and weak and unworthy of her new resolve. Thankfully, she had her cell phone in her hand. She called her automobile club service, and because she was downtown, the helpful service tech was at her side in fifteen minutes.

Annalise shifted restlessly from foot to foot as he slid a device down inside the glass, popped the lock and opened her door. "Thank you," she said fervently. She handed him a fifty-dollar tip. "Take your wife out to dinner on me."

With the man's excited thanks still ringing in her ears, she sprinted for the building and boarded the elevator. She'd been in Sam's condo once before…at a fund-raising reception for the Alzheimer's Foundation. But on that evening, she and Sam had never even exchanged words, even though she'd been aware of him all night.

The elevator clanged to a stop. Annalise stepped out into a hallway carpeted in pewter and burgundy color blocks. Clutching the cake carrier and her purse like a lifeline, she rang the doorbell.

When Sam opened the door, she gaped. Never had she seen him like this…wild-eyed, harried, suspiciously unsurprised. She frowned. "May I come in?" She didn't mention the offering and he didn't seem to notice that she carried an odd accessory.

He kept the door closed except for a barely polite twelve inches. "I saw you park on the street," he said. "Now's not really a good time. I've got—"

A woman appeared at his shoulder, peering into the hall. "Who is it, Sammy? Dinner's almost ready."

Sammy? Dear God. Surely Sam hadn't taken to dating cougars.

He closed his eyes momentarily, a crease forming between his eyebrows. "Annalise, this is my mother, Charlaine Ely. Mom, Annalise Wolff."

"Wolff? Oh, my goodness, come in. I've heard about your family for years, but you know that since my husband and I divorced when Sammy was little, I've rarely been in Charlottesville. It's a pleasure to meet you. One of Sam's old high school friends is here. She's opening a new restaurant soon back in Alabama, and I thought it would be fun to try the menu out on Sam. We're having a casual bite to eat. You're welcome to join us."

With Sam and Annalise acting like cardboard cutouts, the talkative Charlaine ushered them into the kitchen. It was then that Annalise's heart stopped. Because there, standing in front of the stove, and wearing an apron, no less, was Sam's perfect woman.

She was shorter than Annalise, and curvier. Her smile was open and generous, and she seemed right at home in Sam's ultramodern, state-of-the-art kitchen.

After a flurry of introductions, all orchestrated by Sam's mother, *Daphne* spoke up. "The rolls will be ready in five minutes. I hope everyone is hungry."

"Rolls?" The question came from deep inside Annalise's nauseated tummy.

Daphne beamed. "Yeast rolls. My grandma's recipe."

"Oh, goody." Annalise felt her temper rise. Sam had barely left her bed, and already this cross between Martha Stewart and Angelina Jolie was ensconced in his condo. *Jerk.*

Charlaine noticed the cake box. "Oh, lovely. Did you bring dessert? I bought some ice cream, but it will keep. Let me put it on a plate."

Annalise gripped the carrier with all her might. "Um, no. This is for my grandmother. I didn't mean to bring it in."

Sam frowned. "All your grandparents are dead."

"Sam!" Charlaine was shocked. "That was rude." She patted Annalise on the shoulder. "Now don't be intimidated by Daphne. She's a professional, so we can't hope to compete with that. But I'm sure your cake is lovely."

While Annalise watched, mute with mortification, the insistent Charlaine loosened Annalise's fingers one by one and took possession of the cake box. When she set it on the counter and removed the lid, you could have heard a pin drop in the room.

The smell of warm yeast permeated the air, and Annalise wanted to die. All eyes were locked on the chocolate-covered blob. She bit her lip. "Sam mentioned how he always loved white cake with chocolate icing," she mumbled. "When he was growing up. I wanted to thank him for putting me in touch with his grandmother and helping me get the new job."

Daphne leaned over, a lingering horrified fascination in her eyes as she assessed Annalise's very first effort at baking. "I'm sure it tastes good," she said, her cheery voice consoling.

It was the last straw. "I have to go," Annalise croaked. "Sorry to miss dinner." She made a dash for the door, blinking back stupid feminine tears. Her hand was on the knob when Sam stopped her by the sheer expedient of putting his body between her and the exit.

"It's not what you think," he said urgently. "I didn't know they were coming."

She searched his face, trying to read the truth, summoning her courage and refusing to remember the last time she had poured out her heart to this man. "I really need to talk to you," she said. "Tonight."

Sam hesitated. And in that split second, her heart shriveled. Her soul turned to ice.

With all her might, she shoved him out of the way, ripped open the door and ran like hell.

Thirteen

Sam might have had worse days, but he couldn't remember when. With his mother and her guest in his house and a very nice dinner that Daphne had labored over for several hours ready to serve, how could he run out and leave them?

But dear God, Annalise had come to him…of her own free will. And she wanted to talk…tonight. That had to be good. Right? He would gobble down dinner and then go find her. A forty-five-minute delay to satisfy his social obligation was all that stood between him and holding the woman he loved in his arms again.

By the time the dessert course rolled around, Sam knew he had screwed up big-time. All he could think about was the stricken look in Annalise's eyes. It hit him with sick certainty that she must have seen his hesitation to drop everything and follow her as a second rejection.

His mom brought a bowl of ice cream from the kitchen and set it in front of him.

Sam glared at the offending dessert. "I want cake," he said, the words blunt and to the point.

Daphne leapt to her feet. "Of course," she said brightly. "Let me cut you a piece." She returned moments later, carrying a small china dish. "Here you go."

He took his fork, cut off a big bite and shoved it into his mouth. What happened next made his eyes water. The icing tasted like bitter mud, the cake itself was dry and gritty and he found a piece of eggshell that he was forced to spit into a napkin.

The two women stared at him expectantly.

Sam studied his dessert and sighed. He laid down his fork, and stood up. As an afterthought, he picked up his cup of coffee and took a long swig, trying to rinse the taste from his mouth.

"I have to go," he said firmly. "You both are welcome to stay until tomorrow. The guest rooms are ready. But I have other plans tonight. You'll need to excuse me."

Daphne glared at Charlaine. "I told you this was a bad idea." She smiled wryly at her reluctant host. "Sorry, Sam. Your mother can be very persuasive." She walked around the table and kissed him on his cheek. "It was nice to see you. Good luck with your girl."

Charlaine pouted, but she, too, apologized. "Sometimes I get carried away. Please don't tell your dad. Go find that nice Annalise and smooth things out."

Sam gave them a weary smile. "I'll try. But if you don't hear from me by noon tomorrow, you might want to start dragging the river."

The dark humor was a reflection of the knot in his gut. How in the hell had he managed to repeat the biggest mistake of his life? And with the same woman? The last time he had rejected an overture from Annalise Wolff, she hadn't spoken to him for over half a decade. This debacle was infinitely worse. He'd made love to her, fought with her, left her unwillingly and now this. Annalise had come to him to "talk," and he'd let her think that his mother and her guest were more important.

He grabbed his keys and coat and ran downstairs to his car. Annalise could be anywhere, but she had been upset when she left his place, so he was guessing she headed home to hide out.

The building Annalise lived in was high-end and very classy. The doorman and the concierge were both men in their sixties. Fortunately for Sam, he had gone to college with each of their sons. After an exchange of pleasantries, he laid his cards on the table.

"Annalise and I have been seeing each other. We had a fight. I'm pretty sure she's upstairs planning my demise. I would consider it a deep personal favor if you could give me the spare key."

The two older men exchanged glances. The concierge frowned. "I saw her go up. She looked like she'd been crying."

Sam felt about two inches tall. His heart contracted. "It's a long story, but my mom meddled and made Annalise think I was interested in someone else."

The grizzled man muttered. "Mothers. They're amazing, but damn, they can cramp a guy's style. Sorry, Mr. Ely. I know you don't mean any harm. But I could lose my job."

"At least call upstairs and tell her I'm here," Sam urged.

"Okay. I can do that." He picked up the house phone and dialed two digits. His face was unreadable as he carried on a brief conversation.

Still holding the phone in his hand, he looked at Sam. "She said to tell you she doesn't care about her New Year's resolution. You're a lying, cheating, two-faced…"

Sam held up a hand. "I get the picture. Can I talk to her?"

The concierge handed over the phone.

"Hey, Princess. Please let me come upstairs."

It killed him that her voice was hoarse from crying. "No."

"I was going to call you this evening."

"Ha."

"But when I got home, my mom was there with Daphne. I had no idea they were coming, I swear."

"Did you eat her rolls?"

The weird question took him off guard. "Yes."

"They were delicious, right?"

"Yes."

"And my cake?"

An enormous crevasse opened up at his feet. His heart pounding, he wondered what he should say.

The concierge grabbed the phone from his hand. "Oh, for pity's sake, Ms. Annalise. I'm giving him the spare key. You two are on your own."

He hung up and rummaged under the desk for the correct fob. "Good luck, man."

Sam was pretty sure he should have made a plan before he confronted Annalise. Despite the fact that he was known for his diplomatic abilities, he'd sooner face a mountain lion than a pissed-off Wolff daughter.

It would have been nice if her door had been unlocked… perhaps signaling a softening of her anger. But he had to use the key. Quietly, he stepped inside, laying his things on a table near the door. In front of him, the living room and kitchen opened into each other. The mess caused by the cake creation was painfully visible. He gulped and wiped the back of his hand across his damp forehead.

"Where are you, Princess?"

He jumped when she appeared at his elbow. "Where do you think I am? I live here."

She walked past him to the sofa and waved a hand at a nearby chair. "Since you so rudely burst into my home, you might as well say what you came to say. I don't have all evening."

"I'm guessing you do."

She gaped at him. "I beg your pardon?"

He shrugged. "You came over to my house with a peace offering. And you must have known I wouldn't throw you out. Thus, you must not have plans."

Annalise was wearing an old pair of jeans and a UVA sweatshirt. He didn't even know she owned such clothing. Her hair was hanging loose and wavy down her back, and her feet were tucked into thick woolen socks.

She stared at him, eyes cool with disdain. "I dropped off a thank-you gift. Wasn't planning to stay. No big deal."

He got to his feet and paced, unable to be still. "It *is* a big deal. A very big deal." He waved a hand at the kitchen. "You cooked for me."

Color tinted her cheeks. Wariness veiled her true emotions. "An experiment, nothing more. A messy one, at that."

"I did not reject you tonight," he said firmly. "This is nothing like what happened seven years ago."

"Could have fooled me."

He closed his eyes and counted to thirty. Ten was not nearly enough. "You took me by surprise. I had unexpected company. I handled it badly. Besides, you're not exactly blameless in all this. You sent me away, Annalise. Rather coldly. So, I'm sorry about tonight, but I was angry and I didn't expect to see you. Let's call it even."

"Sure," she said carelessly.

Her easy dismissal was suspect, but he decided to take

it at face value since he had a far more complex agenda to get to. "Why did you really come to see me?" he asked, wanting to take her in his arms, but not sure if she was ready to hear what he had to say.

"It was an impulse. You know how I am. I can't really remember."

He took a deep breath. "In that case, I'll do the talking. Whether you believe it or not, I was coming to see you this evening."

Her total lack of expression indicated boredom or disinterest or maybe both. She was mute.

"Don't you want to know why?"

"Will you leave if I say yes?"

His temper snapped. "I wanted to tell you that I love you, damn it…and ask you to marry me."

He'd never imagined yelling those words at a woman in just that way, but his suave, debonair manners had deserted him. Clearly, he should have dressed up his declaration. He might as well have said the weather was nice for all the reaction he got from Annalise.

"Well," he growled between clenched teeth. "It's customary for a woman to respond with something appropriate at this point."

She bent her head, her face obscured by a fall of hair. "Please don't," she said, her voice almost inaudible. "It's no use."

"You have to talk to me, Annalise. Or we'll never find our way out of this mess." He sat down beside her and pulled her into his arms, her head buried on his shoulder. "I promised I would never hurt you again, and today I made you cry. You have no idea how wretched that makes me feel."

Her slender fingers played with one of his buttons. "I

worked up my courage," she said softly. "So I could tell you the truth. And then I saw Daphne."

He hugged her more tightly. "I haven't set eyes on Daphne since we were in high school. She doesn't matter."

"I believe you, but I saw her, Sam. She's your perfect woman. It was blindingly clear to me. Even if you don't want *her,* there will be another Daphne."

"And that's why you came to my house today?"

"No."

He waited, keeping the chains on his impatience. This was too important to screw up now. "Then why?"

A deep sigh made her chest lift and fall. Beneath his touch, her body was warm and pliant. She sat up, scrubbing the hair from her face. Her eyes were puffy and her nose was red. She was still the most beautiful thing he had ever seen.

"Sam, I…"

"What, darlin'? You can tell me anything."

She shrugged, her eyes suspiciously bright. "I love you. I think I always have. You thought I was too young to know my own mind, but I did."

"You don't sound too excited about it," he said, trying to lighten the mood with humor. She looked tragic rather than happy. Perhaps because he had spouted off so much nonsense in the last week. All about his dreams and plans and never once taking into account that to love Annalise Wolff was to love the whole package, a package that didn't fit his requirements and yet somehow was so much more.

He put his hand over her mouth. "Don't say anything else. Not yet." Brushing her cheek with his thumb, he felt his heart seize up in terror at the thought he might have lost her. "If this is about having children, forget it. I want *you,* my love. Nobody else. I don't have to have two-point-five kids and a dog in the country to be happy. All I need is you."

He kissed her softly, a fleeting brush of his lips on hers. "That's why I'm still single at thirty-six. Turns out I wasn't waiting for you to grow up, I was waiting for you to forgive me and offer me another chance."

Tears welled in bright blue eyes, but didn't fall. "I won't let you give up your dream for me, Sam." She cupped his face in her hands. "I want to give you babies. If I can. But you'll have to help me, you'll have to tell me if I do things wrong. If I'm too impatient, or if I'm neglectful of our child."

"Where is this coming from?" She was drawing a scenario that was literally impossible.

Shaking, her face chalky white, she bit her lip. "My mother was a child abuser."

Six words. Six horrible, dreadful words. The stark syllables fell from her lips like stones.

"Oh, my God." This time she was stiff in his arms, too stiff. Fine tremors continued to shiver through her body.

Her whisper was almost inaudible. "She didn't do anything to me. Or if she did, I don't really recall," she said brokenly. "I think Devlyn took the brunt of it. But I remember hiding with my brothers. That was before we went to the mountain, of course. She would drink and she would yell."

"No one interceded?"

"I don't think anyone knew."

"Not even your dad?"

"Maybe. I don't know. But don't you see, it's not just that I grew up without a mother. Even when she was still alive, she was poisoning my mind about what it means to be a loving parent. It's possible that I have inherited her shortcomings."

"That's a load of crap," he said, pushing her away and leaping up from the couch as anger coursed through his veins. The image of a toddler Annalise being knocked around, or even being to scared to come out of hiding, ate at him, curdling his stomach.

He bowed his head. "I know what you're trying to tell me. And it's okay, I swear. The only family I need is you. Not that I think you wouldn't be an amazing mother, but I won't put you through that. Holy hell, Annalise, you've been carrying this around for years. And yet you turned into a beautiful, caring, capable woman. I'm so proud of you, I don't even know how to express it in words."

"Then show me." She stood and joined him. "Tell me that part about loving me again."

He was sick with regret, furious with pain for this delicate and yet incredibly strong Wolff child. "I adore you," he said, the words choked. He held her so tightly, she protested. Relaxing his grip only a bit, he laid his forehead on hers. "I want to marry you. And if we have babies or we don't have babies, it will be a decision we make together. I love you, Annalise."

She reached up to kiss him. The aching hunger that had built inside him since the moment he drove away, leaving her at the farm, coalesced into a white-hot desire that hardened his erection to the point of pain.

Kissing wasn't enough. Feeling her body against his wasn't enough. He had to be in her, on her, devouring her. He stripped her clothes with mad abandon. Annalise sobbed once, her hands ripping at his shirt. "I need you, Sam. So much."

They were naked and tumbled onto the couch before he could speak. "I won't ever let you walk away again. You're mine, Annalise. I'll spend the rest of my life protecting you." He stroked her breasts one at a time, reverently, hungrily. "I know that sounds strange. Since you could probably kick my ass if you wanted to. But just because you've been taught to be tough doesn't mean you can't let down your guard with me. Everyone deserves a safe place…a shelter from the world. I want to be that for you."

He watched her eyes close when he slid inside her body, the fit tight enough to make him catch his breath. "Princess… Tell me you love me. Tell me again."

"I do," she moaned, her legs wrapped about his waist. "Forever. Always."

The sex was different this time, deeper, more powerful, forging a connection that would never be broken. He wouldn't allow it. His climax bore down on him, impossible to resist. "Come for me, my love." He kissed her hard, grinding his hips until he heard her cry out. After that, nothing mattered but Annalise, always Annalise….

When he could breathe again, he lifted her in his arms and carried her down the hall until he found her bedroom. It was bright and eye-catching and unconventional. Much like its owner.

The bed was not made, so he dropped her on the magenta sheet and sprawled beside her. "Can I spend the night?" he asked, yawning.

Annalise grinned. "Your house too full?"

"You could say that."

"Poor Sam."

He skated his fingers over her flat belly, headed south. "I noticed that you didn't answer my marriage proposal."

"You need to be sure, Sam. We've only had one weekend. That's hardly a foundation for a future."

"I've known you my entire life, honey. If things had played out differently, we might have hooked up a long time ago. I probably know more about you than any of the men you've dated. And as for our one naughty weekend, that just seals the deal. A sexual connection like that is rare, Princess. So I'll ask you again. Will. You. Marry me."

She curled onto her side, head propped on her hand. "One question first."

His roving hand stilled, halting just beneath her ribs. The steady beat of her heart reassured him. "Ask me anything."

"How did my cake taste?"

There it was again, that brutally dangerous, gaping hole at his feet. Taking a deep breath, reminding himself of all he knew about his wife-to-be, he grimaced. "It was awful."

She burst into laughter, her vibrant face alight with happiness. "In that case, yes…I'll marry you. Because such brave honesty is rare," she teased. "And I'd be a fool to let you go."

Epilogue

Eighteen months later

Annalise leaned over the counter, putting the finishes touches on a birthday cake for her dad. He'd been thrilled when she and Sam married, and happier still when they'd built Annalise's dream house on Wolff Mountain.

In fact, today was the first official function in the new abode. She gazed around her, seeing Sam's skill and caring in every detail. He'd been absolutely determined to give her everything she wanted.

"Come taste the icing," she called out. "I know the cake part is okay, because I made two just to be sure."

Sam walked in, still buttoning his cuff links. They had decided to do a formal dinner for the entire Wolff clan. "Okay," he said, his face doleful. "Guinea pig reporting for service."

She pinched his arm. "Don't be mean." She scooped her

finger through the icing left in the bowl. "Be honest. I've got a frozen cheesecake I can use as a backup."

Her handsome husband took her hand, sucking two of her fingers into his mouth and licking them clean. "It's perfect." He paused, eyes alight with mischief. "I know how you hate wasting anything. I imagine we could put that leftover icing to good use."

"Behave yourself, Sam." Knees weak, she swallowed hard, reminding herself that their guests were on the way. But the temptation to take up Sam on his wicked offer was almost irresistible.

He released her long enough to dry his hand on a dish towel. "So what did you end up getting him for a present?"

"I didn't." Her mouth dry, she watched his face.

"Why not? I know the old man can buy anything he wants, but he always loves the gifts you pick out for him."

"I thought I'd go nontraditional this year." She pressed her hand to her stomach. "And you helped."

Sam went white as incredulity, joy and fierce triumph raced across his face in quick succession. He scooped her up, whirling her around in a circle. "A baby? You're sure?"

She ruffled his hair, smiling down at him, feeling a wellspring of happiness that never seemed to fade. "In about seven and a half months you're going to be a daddy."

His eyes glistened. "Thank you, Princess." His voice was hoarse. He lowered her to her feet and kissed her with aching sweetness.

She laid her head on his shoulder, chuckling as her arms slid around his waist and squeezed. "In all fairness, you did most of the work."

"I'm hoping for a girl," he confessed softly, stroking her hair in a way that brought tears to Annalise's eyes, tears of inexpressible wonder at the goodness of life.

"Can you handle two of us?" she teased.

"God, I hope so. " He took her hand and lifted her fingers to his lips, kissing them tenderly. "Such news requires a very private celebration. Later. When I have you alone. But for now, my love, please know this. You're my perfect woman. In every way."

* * * * *

#2209 THE KING NEXT DOOR

Kings of California

Maureen Child

Griffin King has strict rules about getting involved with a single mother, but temptation is right next door.

#2210 BEDROOM DIPLOMACY

Daughters of Power: The Capital

Michelle Celmer

A senator's daughter ends up as a bargaining chip that could divert a besotted diplomat's attention to marriage negotiations instead!

#2211 A REAL COWBOY

Rich, Rugged Ranchers

Sarah M. Anderson

He's given up Hollywood for his ranch and doesn't want to go back. How far will she go to sign him to the role of a lifetime?

#2212 MARRIAGE WITH BENEFITS

Winner of Harlequin's 2011 SYTYCW contest

Kat Cantrell

Cia Allende needs a husband—so she can divorce him and gain her trust fund. She doesn't expect that the man she's handpicked will become someone she can't live without.

#2213 ALL HE REALLY NEEDS

At Cain's Command

Emily McKay

When lovers must suddenly work together to unravel a mystery from his family's past, their private affair threatens to become very public.

#2214 A TRICKY PROPOSITION

Cat Schield

When Ming asks her best friend to help her become a mother, he persuades her to conceive the old-fashioned way. But will his brother—Ming's ex-fiancé—stand in the way?

REQUEST YOUR FREE BOOKS!

2 FREE NOVELS PLUS 2 FREE GIFTS!

HARLEQUIN® *Desire*

ALWAYS POWERFUL, PASSIONATE AND PROVOCATIVE

YES! Please send me 2 FREE Harlequin Desire® novels and my 2 FREE gifts (gifts are worth about $10). After receiving them, if I don't wish to receive any more books, I can return the shipping statement marked "cancel." If I don't cancel, I will receive 6 brand-new novels every month and be billed just $4.30 per book in the U.S. or $4.99 per book in Canada. That's a savings of at least 14% off the cover price! It's quite a bargain! Shipping and handling is just 50¢ per book in the U.S. and 75¢ per book in Canada.* I understand that accepting the 2 free books and gifts places me under no obligation to buy anything. I can always return a shipment and cancel at any time. Even if I never buy another book, the two free books and gifts are mine to keep forever.

225/326 HDN FVP7

Name	(PLEASE PRINT)	
Address		Apt. #
City	State/Prov.	Zip/Postal Code

Signature (if under 18, a parent or guardian must sign)

Mail to the Harlequin® Reader Service:
IN U.S.A.: P.O. Box 1867, Buffalo, NY 14240-1867
IN CANADA: P.O. Box 609, Fort Erie, Ontario L2A 5X3

Want to try two free books from another line?
Call 1-800-873-8635 or visit www.ReaderService.com.

* Terms and prices subject to change without notice. Prices do not include applicable taxes. Sales tax applicable in N.Y. Canadian residents will be charged applicable taxes. Offer not valid in Quebec. This offer is limited to one order per household. Not valid for current subscribers to Harlequin Desire books. All orders subject to credit approval. Credit or debit balances in a customer's account(s) may be offset by any other outstanding balance owed by or to the customer. Please allow 4 to 6 weeks for delivery. Offer available while quantities last.

Your Privacy—The Harlequin® Reader Service is committed to protecting your privacy. Our Privacy Policy is available online at www.ReaderService.com or upon request from the Harlequin Reader Service.

We make a portion of our mailing list available to reputable third parties that offer products we believe may interest you. If you prefer that we not exchange your name with third parties, or if you wish to clarify or modify your communication preferences, please visit us at www.ReaderService.com/consumerschoice or write to us at Harlequin Reader Service Preference Service, P.O. Box 9062, Buffalo, NY 14269. Include your complete name and address.

Navy SEAL Blake Landon joins this year's
parade of *Uniformly Hot!* military heroes in
Tawny Weber's

A SEAL's Seduction

Blake's lips brushed over Alexia's and she forgot that they were
on a public beach. His breath was warm, his lips soft.

The fingertips he traced over her shoulder were like a gentle
whisper. It was sweetness personified. She felt like a fairy-tale
princess being kissed for the first time by her prince.

And he was delicious.

Mouthwatering, heart-stopping delicious. And clearly he
had no problem going after what he wanted, she realized as he
slid the tips of his fingers over the bare skin of her shoulder.
Alexia shivered at the contrast of his hard fingertips against
her skin. Her breath caught as his hand shifted, sliding lower,
hinting at but not actually caressing the upper swell of her
breast.

Her heart pounded so hard against her throat, she was surprised it didn't jump right out into his hand.

She wanted him. As she'd never wanted another man in
her life. For years, she'd behaved. She'd carefully considered
her actions, making sure she didn't hurt others. She'd poured
herself into her career, into making sure her life was one she
was proud of.

And she already had a man who wanted her in his life. A nice, sweet man she could talk through the night with and never run out of things to say.

But she wanted more.

She wanted a man who'd keep her up all night. Who'd drive her wild, sending her body to places she'd never even dreamed of.

Even if it was only for one night.

And that, she realized, was the key. One night of crazy. One night of delicious, empowered, indulge-her-every-desire sex, with a man who made her melt.

One night would be incredible.

One night would *have* to be enough.

Pick up *A SEAL's Seduction* by Tawny Weber, on sale January 22.

Evangeline is surprised when her past lover turns out to be her fiancé's brother. How will she manage the one she loved and the one she has made a deal with?

Follow her path to love January 22, 2013, with

THE ONE THAT GOT AWAY

by Kelly Hunter

"The trouble with memories like ours," he said roughly, "is that you think you've buried them, dealt with them, right up until they reach up and rip out your throat."

Some memories were like that. But not all. Sometimes memories could be finessed into something slightly more palatable.

"Maybe we could try replacing the bad with something a little less intense," she suggested tentatively. "You could try treating me as your future sister-in-law. We could do polite and civil. We could come to like it that way."

"Watching you hang off my brother's arm doesn't make me feel civilized, Evangeline. It makes me want to break things."

Ah.

"Call off the engagement." He wasn't looking at her. And it wasn't a request. "Turn this mess around."

"We need Max's trust fund money."

"I'll cover Max for the money. I'll buy you out."

"What?" Anger slid through her, hot and biting. She could feel her composure slipping away but there was nothing else for it. Not in the face of the hot mess that was Logan. "No," she said as steadily as she could. "No one's buying me out of anything, least of all MEP. That company is *mine,* just as much as it is Max's. I've put six years into it, eighty-hour weeks of blood, sweat, tears and fears into making it the success it is. Prepping it for bigger opportunities, and one of those opportunities is just around the corner. Why on earth would I let you buy me out?"

He meant to use his big body to intimidate her. Closer, and closer still, until the jacket of his suit brushed the silk of her dress, but he didn't touch her, just let the heat build. His lips had that hard sensual curve about them that had haunted her dreams for years. She couldn't stop staring at them.

She needed to stop staring at them.

"You can't be in my life, Lena. Not even on the periphery. I discovered that the hard way ten years ago. So either you leave willingly…or I make you leave."

Find out what Evangeline decides to do by picking up THE ONE THAT GOT AWAY by Kelly Hunter. Available January 22, 2013, wherever Harlequin books are sold.